MERMAIDS

MERMAIDS

PATTY DANN

1 ◆ 9 ◆ 8 ◆ 6

TICKNOR & FIELDS ◆ NEW YORK

Library of Congress Cataloging-in-Publication Data

Dann, Patty.
Mermaids.

I. Title.
PS3554.A575M4   1986   813'.54   86-5891
ISBN 0-89919-471-0

PRINTED IN THE UNITED STATES OF AMERICA

S 10 9 8 7 6 5 4 3 2 1

To my parents

In 1212 A.D. thousands of children left their families to join what is now known as the Children's Crusade. It is said that they were followed by clouds of butterflies and schools of fish.

1963

I

𐆌

Mrs. flax was happiest when she was leaving a place, but I wanted to stay put long enough to fall down crazy and hear the Word of God. I always called my mother Mrs. Flax. She had driven my little sister Kate and me in the blue Buick station wagon for three days this time, racing from Oklahoma to New England. Skinny Burt LeForest, who had a bulging Adam's apple and was in my high school, tore behind us in a truck full of our furniture, driving wildly to keep up. I had seen Mrs. Flax kiss Burt by the stove a week before, when he came by to change a light bulb we couldn't reach.

We arrived in Grove on a round-moon night, with lilacs blowing sweet against our new house in the breeze. We rented the place; we always rented. I lay in the back seat, holding Kate, with her curly red hair, on top of me as I stared up at the windshield, which was still covered with Oklahoma dust. Mrs. Flax turned off the motor. I shut my eyes and prayed this would be the town where I heard a voice. Joan of Arc heard voices at thirteen; I had just turned fourteen, but I hadn't given up hope.

"But Charlotte," Mrs. Flax said when she found me at

age six, kneeling in the middle of the kitchen on a hot Arizona afternoon, "Charlotte, you're Jewish." Mrs. Flax didn't believe in ritual or tradition. "Religion weighs me down," she said. I, however, decided I wanted to repent the first time I saw a girl with ashes on her forehead cross herself and chant Hail Marys before a spelling bee. That was when we lived in Wisconsin; the next day I stole an old piece of charcoal from a neighbor man's barbecue and walked around with a smudge between my eyebrows for a week and a half.

I was eight years old when Mrs. Flax was pregnant with Kate. While she drove with her belly pressed up against the steering wheel, I knelt way in the back of the station wagon. I solemnly clipped two curls of my hair and placed them in the Cracker Jacks box where I saved my baby teeth. I prayed these relics would be kissed by miles of crusaders, who would wait piously in line someday.

I always had trouble trying to be holy, though. First of all, I liked to lie a lot; second of all, I kept falling in love.

Mrs. Flax climbed the porch steps in her high heels and polka dot dress. "Girls," she called out into the night, "come give this nice young man a hand."

People said Mrs. Flax and I looked alike — green eyes, dark curly hair, medium height; not that we ever were the kind to stand giggling back to back. I listened to Burt drag boxes and furniture inside. New England was only a donkey-head shape on the map to me. I hadn't come across a Massachusetts saint so far; I didn't know what the odds would be — not that I knew anything about odds, but I prayed this would be the place where I'd find divine inspiration.

"Wake up, Kate," I said finally. "Welcome to home sweet home number eighteen."

Kate woke up yawning, with her hands over her ears. I adored Kate; everybody did. When she was born, I wanted to name her Gobnet, after the virgin beekeeper saint. "I worry, Charlotte, I really do," said Mrs. Flax.

Kate hopped up the steps on one foot and I followed her onto the porch. Burt was trying to lift the couch up onto his shoulders and through the front door. I held my breath, trying not to breathe in Mrs. Flax's perfume, as I clutched a leg of the couch; I didn't believe in perfume or make-up or anything artificial. I washed with icy water whenever I could stand it; I was going to lead a pure life, free of sin. After Burt yanked the couch up through the doorway, Mrs. Flax followed him inside.

I held Kate's hand and stared sleepily out at the dark yard, breathing in the pine air. It seemed as if we'd been on the road forever. I had calculated that I'd wasted far too much of my life in a car. No saints, either male or female, had ever heard the Word at seventy miles an hour on the interstate. I needed to stand very still and as quiet as possible, and then inspiration would pour through my soul. I was losing patience, though. I had tried to be charitable, taking care of Kate all the time and trying not to kill my mother, but lately I was worried I'd succumb to a life of sin. Lots of saints had led secular lives before they turned to the monastic path; I just wasn't sure. I'd read everything to find the answer — the Bible, both the Old Testament and the New, and every book I could find on martyrdom. In sixth grade, while a circle of girls sat around reading horse books, I sat alone at my desk, reading about Simone Weil, the Jewish girl who starved her head off trying to become a saint.

Suddenly Mrs. Flax gave one of her loud laughs, and a few moments later Burt was back outside. He slapped me on the shoulder, then jumped off the porch and into his truck and drove off down the road. As soon as he left, I took Kate inside. The place smelled of tomato sauce and toy trains. Burt had struck the couch in the middle of the living room, and there was a jumble of boxes piled in front of the fireplace. Our room was down the hall, with bunk beds set up against the wall. Kate climbed onto the top bunk right away; she liked the top because she said it was like floating on water. I always preferred to be close to the ground.

I wandered through the house, avoiding Mrs. Flax, who was sitting on the counter next to the sink, humming "The Star Spangled Banner." I stared at the double bed in her room, trying to figure out if she'd done it with old Burt; she seemed to do it with everyone else. I considered stealing the car right then and running away forever. Within the last year, Mrs. Flax had taught me how to drive. I was underage, but she said being able to drive was the most important skill a woman could have; she taught me one morning in Oklahoma at five A.M., behind the supermarket, as the orange sun came up. I was a slow driver, a very slow driver, driving as if there was something wrong with my mind, according to Mrs. Flax; I put on my signal lights miles before I turned. If there was a church in Grove, I knew I'd be able to drive there if I wanted, but I'd decided long ago that church was not the place for divine inspiration. Saints were called while they were out herding sheep or staggering around the desert or down at the river, getting water in a bucket. Saints were not called while listening to a hot-faced man yell at them. I walked down the hall, past a room with RED SOX carved into the door. The floor was covered with boxes of Mrs. Flax's personal possessions, which she had decided bored her to tears.

When I got back to our room, Kate was curled up like a snail, sound asleep, with her dress on; but I could never sleep the first night in a place. I never could sleep until I made the room look like it did in every previous house. I opened one of the boxes Burt had dumped in the corner and carefully took out Kate's rock collection. I dusted the rocks twice, then laid them out on a low shelf against the wall. Kate was crazy about those rocks. She picked them up wherever we lived. Now there were a good number stuck to cardboard. Her method was to wrap adhesive tape around each rock, then label it with a made-up name. The large rocks were too heavy to glue to cardboard, though. Those she just labeled and lined up in a shoebox, like fat sailors with their white belts.

I took out Kate's swimming trophies, which I'd wrapped individually in towels at our last house. I dusted them off and lined them in a row on the window ledge. Then I took out my old Cracker Jacks box, which I'd dragged all over America. I hadn't opened it in six years; I held my breath, then ripped the top and emptied the relics into my hand. As the years passed and we'd moved from state to state, the baby teeth had turned yellow and the curls now lay like dry apostrophes, and still God had not spoken to me. I put them back in the Cracker Jacks box and leaned the box next to Kate's *Children's Encyclopedia of Fish of the World* on the shelf.

Then I took out the torn picture of a pair of grown-up brown tie shoes on yellow grass that I was certain belonged to my father. Kate had a different father, but I never told her that; it was one of those lies I just kept telling and telling. I didn't know if it was to protect Kate or because I liked to have secrets, but I always lied. Mrs. Flax never corrected me, either. When I was a kid I liked to refer to my father as Our Father Who Art in Heaven, and when Kate learned to talk baby talk she called him by the same name. I wondered every minute if my father was ever coming back. Saint Barbara became a Christian while her father was away; she became a hermit and lived in a bathhouse. When her father came back he almost killed her for becoming a Christian, but then he was struck by lightning and died with a sizzled smile on his face. My father called Mrs. Flax a few times a year, but he never introduced himself to me. Men called Mrs. Flax every day of her life, and I drove myself nuts trying to figure out which one was Dad. Every few months Mrs. Flax said he'd be visiting soon, but the guy hadn't made an appearance yet.

I found a thumbtack on the floor and stuck the picture of his shoes to the closet door. I kissed the picture, then kissed Kate's curls, which smelled faintly of chlorine. Then I lay down on the lower bunk and tried to sleep, but I kept remembering a pair of hands, which might have been my father's. When I was younger than Kate, in a town in Idaho, a man slid a pair of cardboard glasses on my face, lightly touching my ears, so I could watch an eclipse of the sun without going blind. I stood backward at the window, holding Mrs. Flax's powdery compact mirror, trying to see the sun, but all I could see was my own mouth. And then those hands lightly took the glasses away.

I liked the new house and I prayed we wouldn't be leaving right away. I prayed I would stop lying all the time. I prayed my father would return. I prayed I wouldn't fall crazy in love so much, and then I prayed that I would.

The phone rang early the next morning, and I was the one who stumbled out of bed to the kitchen to answer it after twelve rings. Mrs. Flax always insisted on having the phone connected before she moved into a place so she wouldn't miss a single gentleman caller. A man with a faraway voice that sounded like potatoes asked if my mother was home. I thought it could have been the guy who planted his seed, but I couldn't tell. Mrs. Flax finally got to the phone and sat on the kitchen table, pulling her bathrobe around her, then letting it fall open as she crossed her leg, swinging it back and forth. She wouldn't give a clue who it was, though. All I knew was I'd never seen her so friendly at that hour of the morning. The only people she consistently liked, aside from Kate, were Avon ladies; it was true wherever we lived.

Before we moved to Grove I had almost begun to think I was going to graduate in Oklahoma; not that I loved the place, not that I liked squinting until I'd go blind, and not that I liked the taste of dust when I licked my lips, but we'd lived there longer than anywhere else. Then Mrs. Flax began dating her boss, and although the pattern wasn't predictable, it often meant we'd be moving soon. A few days later she came home from work early one afternoon, ran a bath, and sat splashing around, hitting her fists on the water. She reached under the sink for the atlas, opened it up, and placed a dripping finger down on Grove. The next day she dialed information and found the name of Pine & Timber Realtor and spoke to Linda Jenkins, who had never dealt with a long-distance tenant before.

Mrs. Flax hung up the phone after talking to the man with the potato voice and stood gripping the sink, with her back to me.

"Would you kindly see if Kate has fallen out of bed again?" she said as she opened the empty refrigerator.

"Who was that? Was that him?"

Kate appeared in the doorway, rubbing her eyes, wearing the wrinkled dress she had slept in. "Do they give us food in this place?"

"Not yet, baby, we'll go to the store later," said Mrs. Flax. "But I have some candy bars in my purse."

This is probably the best time to say a word about Mrs. Flax and food. The word is hors d'oeuvres. That's all the woman cooked. *Fun Finger Foods* was her main source book, except for when Kate was a baby and we lived on *Hors d'Oeuvres for Your Infant*, which she found at a tag sale in El Paso.

Anyway, that first morning in Grove we ate Mars Bars, sitting on the kitchen table because old Burt had forgotten to pack the chairs.

"The Pilgrims live here," said Kate, swinging her legs. "My teacher said they sleep on a rock near here."

There was a knock on the door and Mrs. Flax slid off the table. "I hate Pilgrims," she said as she went to see who was there.

I ran to the window; there was a man, a tall man with black hair and the smoothest skin I'd ever seen, standing on the porch. I remember I thought he looked like a pirate. Although it was warm out, he was wearing a thick sweater and heavy corduroy pants, and he had Indian moccasins on his feet.

"Ma'am," he said, pressing his forehead to the screen door.

" 'Ma'am'?" said Mrs. Flax through the screen. "What can I do for you, sir?"

"I work up the hill. My name is Joe Peretti and I just wondered if you got moved in all right."

"And what is up the hill, Mr. Joe Peretti?"

"The convent, Protectors of the Blessèd Souls."

I crossed myself and leaned against the refrigerator. "This is a sign," I whispered. "This is a real sign."

Mrs. Flax opened the door wide. "If I need you, I'll call, thank you. How old did you say you were?"

"Twenty-nine," said Joe.

"Well, there is one thing, the porch swing. Would you mind putting it up? I can't reach."

Joe cleared his throat, and Mrs. Flax stood inside at the living room window, strumming her fingernails along the Venetian blinds, while Joe fumbled with the chains of the squeaking swing.

That night we were sitting on the kitchen table, eating little gems called Cheese-Ball Pick-Me-Ups and Wagon-ho Miniature Franks, with toothpicks, when Mrs. Flax said, "That Mr. Joe Peretti is a most attractive man."

Kate giggled something about him looking like Joe Poseidon, King of the Sea, who was her favorite god, but I threw my toothpick on the floor.

"Don't you think so, Charlotte?" said Mrs. Flax. "You're old enough to have a boyfriend now, don't you think?"

"If I'm old enough, maybe you're too old," I said and walked out of the kitchen.

I had never actually had a boyfriend, although I'd fallen in love ninety-one times so far. Once at a pep rally in the crowded gymnasium in Oklahoma, when everyone was jumping up and down, a small group of boys bumped into me on purpose and touched my breasts. I had always been embarrassed about not being flat-chested; I wanted to be flat and strong like Joan of Arc going into battle, but I was getting as many curves as Mrs. Flax. I'd fallen in love with every single one of the male teachers I'd ever had, especially the history teachers. I loved to hear them talk about Hannibal as if they knew what they were talking about, as if they knew what it was like to cross the Alps on elephants who had snow in their ears. I lay down on my bed and put the pillow over my face. I wanted to be a virtuous person. I wanted to have a holy soul, but I was beginning to doubt I had a prayer.

"What do you think, Charlotte?" called Mrs. Flax. "D'you think it's Divine Providence that our nearest next-door neighbors are nuns?"

Mrs. Flax's parents had been bakers in Poland, and when they moved to America they opened the first kosher bakery in Minerva, Ohio. As a child, Mrs. Flax had stood in the kitchen by the oven, twisting pieces of dough into messy, uncookable knots. She thought cooking bread was pointless, let alone cooking kosher. Her oldest sister was the one who stayed home and later took over the bakery, but Mrs. Flax left town on the last day of high school. The night before, she had stood in her parents' kosher kitchen, eating a ham sandwich and a glass of milk and making her mother cry.

The next morning I got up at sunrise when I heard a bell ringing from up the hill, and I put on a navy blue dress. I always wore dresses, never pants. If I ever went on a crusade I'd wear pants, but I thought a truly holy person should try to be proper at all times. I also wore a pair of beige vinyl boots. The boots were the only thing my father ever sent me; they arrived in a ripped box one day from California. They were ugly, I knew that, they had no grace, but they were a gift from him, and I wore them as often as I could stand it. I was always too hot, and the boots made my heels sore, but I thought it was best to always be slightly in pain, as an act of penance for my sins.

I walked across the yard full of daffodils and started up the steep hill to the convent. I tried to walk on tiptoe the whole way so I wouldn't disturb the nuns. At the top of the hill was a wrought-iron gate with a sign that said NO TRESPASSERS ALLOWED. The gate was open, though, and I could see three nuns walking by the bell tower, their heads bent in prayer. I'd seen a convent once before, when we lived in Oregon when I was very young. My class had gone on a field trip, and a forest ranger made me count out loud the rings of a giant sequoia tree. On the way home we stopped for a picnic in a field outside the convent.

That first time I saw nuns, they were playing horseshoes. A bunch of them were standing in a crooked black line on the lawn, laughing as each one threw into the sky and missed. Rusty horseshoes landed all over the grass. When the game was over, the nuns zigzagged across the lawn, scooped up the horseshoes, and dropped them, clanging, into a wood box. Then the nuns picked up their prayer books from a neat stack in the shade of a tree and walked away in rows of black skirts, chanting Latin. "My mommy and daddy are in fifth grade. My mommy and daddy are in fifth grade," I thought they said.

I walked through the gate of the Protectors of the Blessèd Souls, whispering "Trespass not against those who trespass against you," and felt suddenly calm as I entered the grounds. It was a bursting spring day, all the blossoms were out, the dogwood and apple, and the lawns were freshly cut. I snuck across the grass, past the bell tower, to the stone chapel with stained red and yellow windows. I put my ear to the oak door but I didn't hear a sound. As a child, I once spent an hour with my ear pressed to the door of some nuns' car in a shopping center, but all I heard was a loudspeaker blaring "Swiss steaks, two for the price of one."

I walked deeper into the convent, back on a curving path through the woods. I hid behind a tree when I heard the sound of digging in the ground. I was scared I'd discovered secret catacombs, but when I squinted my eyes I could see a man kneeling in a vegetable garden, surrounded by small tomato plants. He had his back to me, but I could see it was Joe Peretti, Joe Poseidon Peretti himself. I shut my eyes. "Dear God," I prayed, "don't let me fall in love and want to do disgusting things." I watched him dig up weeds, then throw them off into the woods. "Dear God," I prayed, "I love the way he throws." When Joe stood up I held my breath, but he didn't walk toward me; he walked the other way. The second he was gone I missed him, I swear. I wrapped my arms around the tree and pressed my ear to the rough wood. A few minutes later I heard something being dragged along the ground, and I ducked behind the tree to watch. Joe was returning with a sledge hammer and long wooden stakes in one hand and a large roll of chicken wire in the other. This is it, I thought. I'm going to be tortured by rods and rack and fire, just like Saint Agatha. I watched Joe all morning, digging deep holes for the stakes, then pounding them into the ground. He covered his precious tomato plants with chicken wire, pricking his fingers until they were beaded with blood. Then he suddenly began ripping the wire away from the stakes. He looked like he was having a fit; I wanted to run over to him and lick his fingers and ask if he was having supernatural revelations. He threw everything to the ground, then stormed off the other way. I leaned against the tree and crossed myself; I decided I'd wait forever for him to return.

2

I STAYED AWAY from the convent for the
rest of the summer as an act of penance. I hadn't seen Joe
since that morning in the woods. Mrs. Flax found a job
right away, working for one of the two lawyers in town,
and Kate spent every day swimming her head off in the
T-shaped public pool. I was so bored I considered running
off to the desert and living on dates and berries. The only
excitement was listening to Joe ring the bell in the tower,
at dawn, at noon, at dusk, then at night when the nuns were
supposed to be in bed. Men called for Mrs. Flax around the
clock and I began asking for their first, middle, and last
names, but I didn't have a lead on where my father was
hiding out. I thought there was a chance I'd end up a house-
wife saint, like Martha, sister of Lazarus; I spent hours
vacuuming, praying the Word of God would crash through
the house as I reached for a snarl of lint under the bed. But
nothing happened the whole stupid summer and finally
September arrived.

School began on a day that could have been summer; I
stuck to my vows, though, and wore a heavy corduroy

dress and my boots. Mrs. Flax went off to work early and Kate got a ride to elementary school in a yellow van with smiling faces painted on the sides, so I stood alone in the front yard, waiting to be picked up. The pencil-colored bus arrived at quarter to eight; when I saw all those eyes jammed to the windows, I considered collapsing on the ground, on the chance that a spring would suddenly burst forth where I fell. I tried to be calm but I stumbled on the bottom step when I saw who the bus driver was. It was Joe, Joe Poseidon from the convent. I walked straight to the back of the bus and bent my head to my book of women saints, pretending to read about Rose of Lima, of Lima, Peru.

I got through the first day, feeling the vague homesickness I always felt at school. First days I always fled to the bathroom and hid in one of the stalls; it was a ritual of mine that helped me survive first days across the land. On a first day when I was nine in Tennessee, I found a gold cross on a chain on the floor. I washed it off and wore it around my neck, putting it in my mouth whenever I felt like screaming something wild. But several days later, the girl who lost the cross asked me to kindly hand it over.

Mary O'Brien had the locker next to mine at Grove High. She was small and flat-chested, with freckles splattered all over her face. She whispered into her open locker at the end of the first day of school, "Did you have a boyfriend where you used to live or what?"

"Sure, I had two," I said. "Cousins, identical."

"Boys are the best, they really are," said Mary. "Sex is the best, don't you think?"

"Oh, sure. It's the best invention so far."

On the bus home Joe again was the bus driver, and I

again walked straight to the back. As the other kids were dropped off, I realized our house was the last stop on the route; I bent my head again and tried to read about Saint Urith of Chittlehampton.

When everyone else had gotten off the bus, so all the seats were empty between us, Joe looked into the mirror and said, "Hello there, I grew up in your house, you know."

"What?" I whispered, and then, "What?" just loud enough for him to hear. I wondered if he was talking in tongues.

"You can move up if you want," said Joe, adjusting the mirror.

I picked up my books and walked slowly to the front of the bus. I sat down right behind him; he smelled of burning leaves and I wanted to kiss his smooth neck.

"Why did you move?" I said.

"Parents died."

"Oh, sorry." I turned and looked out the window.

"I was born under the kitchen table," he said.

God strike me down, I thought. Born under the kitchen table was almost as good as being born in a manger. Joe said he'd played tight end in high school and I said football was probably my most favorite thing in the world. He said his three older sisters all got married in one year, bing, bing, bing, to a family of brothers and moved to Florida. He'd just started the job in the convent after he'd sold the house to Pine & Timber, but he'd been driving the bus for years. When his mother died he sat on his bed for two days, holding her sweater, which smelled of tomato sauce and the perfume she always wore. "Like violets," he said. Then he said something happened, just like his knee, something snapped. He didn't even care about the Red Sox anymore.

"Who needs them," I said. "I'm sick of the guys." Give me strength not to sit on his lap, I thought. This man used to sleep every night in my own house in the room with RED SOX engraved on the door. I stared at his hand on the gear shift and tried not to imagine him unbuttoning my dress. When we drove up to the house, the house that belonged to both of us, I stood up and put a small smile on my face and tried to look like a nun.

A pink Impala was parked behind the station wagon in the driveway.

"That's Carrie," said Joe, as he opened the door of the bus. "She's an Avon lady now, went to school with my middle sister," and then he smiled at me in the mirror. I tried to look like the Blessèd Virgin as I stepped off the bus.

Carrie was sitting next to Mrs. Flax on the couch when I walked in. Carrie's hair was dyed a red color and she wore a pink chiffon scarf around her neck. She smelled of perfume, hair spray, nail polish, make-up, and air freshener, and she held a pink plastic cosmetics case on her lap.

"Hi, honey," she said. "I was just telling your mother that I love fall. There are four kinds of people in the world, just like the seasons. Know your colors and know your fabrics, that's what I tell my little girls."

Kate walked in from the bedroom, and Carrie said, "I'd kill to have your hair, honey. I hear you're quite a swimmer. Well, that's fine for your figure but it dries out your skin and can damage, really damage that beautiful hair. How old are you?"

"Six," said Kate, rubbing her chlorine eyes.

"Well, I'm all for aquatics, but our hair is our trademark so we've got to protect it."

Mrs. Flax let Carrie dab creams and colors on one side

of her face while Kate sat down between them on the couch. I stood watching in the doorway. I wanted to ask her Joe's story. I wanted to know what the deal was with this beautiful man.

"Now make up the other side of your face, just the way I've done it," said Carrie, but Mrs. Flax said she really wasn't in the mood and sat there like a court jester, with half her face painted. She did buy things, though — she always did — a perfume called "Occur" and a bunch of lipsticks named after flavors of ice cream.

"How about you, honey?" Carrie pointed a lipstick at me. "You look like you'd like to try some color."

I smiled and stepped toward Carrie, but Mrs. Flax shook her head and said, "This one's planning to be a nun."

I walked into my room and slammed the door. I pressed my ear to the wall, listening to Carrie try to change the subject by talking about Mrs. Crain, the school psychologist, who was married to my history teacher. "She could use a new rinse in that crew cut she calls a French wave," Carrie said, but Mrs. Flax said she wanted to know more about the caretaker man in the convent.

"Oh, Joey," said Carrie and laughed. She said Joey was always the handsomest boy in town and didn't Mrs. Flax think he had the best head of hair she'd ever seen. They both laughed, then Carrie said he was one of the most popular boys in high school, on the football team and all, but in the middle of the season senior year he lost it — couldn't run at all. There were two theories in town: some people said it was because his girlfriend, who moved away, went up to Canada and had a baby, and some people said she went to the city for an abortion. Carrie said she personally believed there was a Joey, Jr., walking around somewhere, although Joe had told her the girl was never pregnant at all. Carrie said whatever happened she still thought he had the best legs in New England, and if she wasn't married to such a son-of-a-gun and he wasn't the little brother of her once best friend, she would have thought twice. Then Mrs. Flax said something about younger men being the only hope for the human race.

I heard Kate jumping up and down on the couch, asking for something to use in "big water," which she was always talking about. Carrie asked her if she'd like a bunch of miniature lipsticks, but Kate said what she really wanted was some kind of heavy cream or grease. Mrs. Flax explained that Kate was planning to swim across the English Channel some day and was looking for something to coat her body to protect her from sharks and jellyfish. Carrie said she wasn't sure if she had the exact lotion Kate was looking for, but she did find an old jar of green paste, which was meant to be used for crow's-feet and never really caught on.

Before Carrie left she knocked on my door. "Honey," she said, "you know, you have special eyes. And your eyebrows, only you and Liz Taylor could get away with those."

I knelt at my bed and prayed. "I'd like to be a striptease artist. Please, Lord, forgive me for my sins."

Every day that week I sat right behind Joe, staring at his smooth neck, breathing in his burning-leaves smell, after the other kids were dropped off. In the mornings I sat in the back of the bus, pretending to be a stranger, but in the afternoons we talked. I had decided he'd entered the convent for the sin of getting a girl pregnant. He was a penitent man, which made me love him even more. On Friday afternoon, just before he opened the door, he crossed his hands on the steering wheel and quietly asked if I'd like to go to the shore with him that Sunday, on his day off. He wanted to take pictures of egrets flying south.

"Thank you, I love egrets," I said as I tripped down the steps of the bus. I'd never gone on a date before.

Just before I went to bed that night, I leaned against the stove and asked Mrs. Flax for permission to go on a photographic safari with Joe Peretti.

"Why didn't you tell me that man was your bus driver?" she said. She opened the refrigerator, then slammed it shut. "Charlotte," she said, "I don't give a goddamn where you go."

I couldn't sleep that night. I lay on my back, staring up at Kate's bunk. I didn't want to be like Mrs. Flax; I wanted to be virtuous. But with half of her chromosomes, I didn't know what I was supposed to do. She rarely talked about the past, but she did tell me the bare facts one afternoon, driving across Kansas in the heat, while Kate was asleep on my lap.

When Mrs. Flax left home after high school, she moved to Chicago, where she took a job as a secretary in a hospital. With her first paycheck she bought her first polka dot dress and her first pair of high, high heels and wore them to work the next day. She always liked polka dot dresses and always had at least one in her closet. After six months at the hospital, she bought her first secondhand car and was stopped for the first time for speeding, but, as happened about half the time in following years, she smiled at the policeman and he let her go.

After several hospital jobs in Chicago, she decided she was a poet in her soul and enrolled in night school writing class. She had no natural gift but filled notebooks with angry, unrhymed verse about natural juices and the importance of a passionate life. One night after class, the boy who sat next to her, who was only sixteen and taking his diploma at night so he could work in his father's jewelry store during the day, a slight boy with eyebrows that met in the middle over his dark eyes, looked up at Mrs. Flax in her high heels and told her he liked her poems. Mrs. Flax didn't actually like the boy, although she did like the fact he liked her. She had divided men up into two categories: those who were interesting but treated other people badly, and those who were boring but were kind to other people. This boy, who was two years younger than she was, she married, and he was very considerate of her for a brief time. They shared a one-room apartment, where if she stood tiptoe on a chair she could see Lake Michigan.

But when Mrs. Flax was lying on a delivery table about to give birth in the worst hail storm in five hundred years in Chicago, Mr. Flax stole her car and drove off in a clatter of ice stones. Mrs. Flax considered leaving me at the hospital, sneaking me back into the sterile room with all the newborns and never seeing me again. She spent the next eight years at typing jobs across the country. She had a number of cars and a large number of men and she made it a rule for herself never to be left by anybody again.

On a winter day in Minneapolis, Mrs. Flax gave birth to Kate, whom she and I worshipped. As a child, I liked to pretend Kate was my own and tried to make her call me Mommy. I tickled Kate's baby ears as she lay in her basinette and called her O Holy Innocent. I washed her in the plastic tub much better than Mrs. Flax ever could or wanted to. The only thing Mrs. Flax and I ever did agree on was that Kate was a wonderful child. We both would do anything for her, and when she learned to swim, when most babies were still gnawing on the sides of their playpens, it was just about the only time we ever smiled at each other, across the steamy pool at the YMCA. It was true Kate was an angelic child and a lovely little girl, and she was ecstatic whenever she was in the water.

Kate's father was a nice young man, as Mrs. Flax called him. I never met him, but he'd been in St. Louis for swim races at a hotel where she had a job as a chambermaid for one week. The races being held at the hotel were supposedly to determine whether the nice young man would be headed for the Olympics, and when Mrs. Flax came to deliver clean towels she stayed longer than she should have. She lost her job that day, and the nice young man lost the race, but she did have Kate, who inherited her father's abilities in the water.

Mrs. Flax usually said that talking about the past or staying too long in one place was a waste. "It's all death," she said, as she raced through traffic in the station wagon.

3

At FIVE O'CLOCK on Sunday morning, I
sat tallying my evil thoughts for the week as I swung on
the squeaking porch swing; Joe was late. Mrs. Flax always said if a man was late it was time to clear the deck, but
I was trying to be as patient as Saint Bridget, lady-in-
waiting to Queen Blanche of Namur. By the time Joe drove
up to the mailbox in his old brown Ford, I'd had no revelations; I ran across the damp lawn as fast as possible to the
car. I sat as far away from Joe as I could, pressing my ear
hard against the window until I thought my head would
fall off. Ave Maria, Ave Maria, I sang to myself as we drove
through the sleeping town; I wanted to scream out the
window like a maniac that I was running away with the
caretaker man, but I made a small cross sign over my lips
and tried to shut up. All Joe said, after ten minutes on the
highway, was "breakfast" and swerved off at a truck stop.
We went inside and I stood by the cash register, sticking
out my chest, hoping the truckers would think I was Joe's
sweetheart for life. The yellow-haired waitress winked at
Joe as she handed me a grease-stained bag of glazed dough-

nuts. "That your kid, handsome?" she said, and I considered throwing the doughnuts in her face.

Back in the car, Joe took a plaid thermos of milk from under the seat; we drove along the highway, passing the thermos back and forth. Each time he handed it to me I tried to put my lips exactly where his had been; when he wasn't looking I ran my tongue around the rim.

"I disconnected the speedometer," Joe said, "so you won't think I'm driving too fast."

"Don't worry," I said, "after my mother, nothing is fast."

"She seems like quite a woman," said Joe.

"Yes," I said, "she's a wonderful mom."

Joe asked me if back in June I was the person he saw one morning when he was figuring out a way to keep the deer away from his tomatoes. I said no, I didn't know what he was talking about, I never saw anybody touch chicken wire in my life. Joe didn't seem to care if I was telling the truth; he was the kind of guy who wanted to tell the story of his life. I thought if I could get him going he'd tell some secrets about the nuns. He drove with one hand loosely on the wheel, looking like a movie star, as he told me how the deer were driving him crazy so he'd gone to the old caretaker for advice. The old caretaker pretended he had his own place in town, but he really spent every night at Aunt Sammy's house. Aunt Sammy was a woman who everyone called a witch. Joe had seen her only one Halloween when he was a kid, when he and his sisters dared to show up at her house because everyone said she made the best caramel candies. On that long ago Halloween, Joe dressed up as a pumpkin-headed soldier and had to wheel his pumpkin head around in a wheelbarrow because it weighed so much. His sisters had gone dressed as triplets. Aunt Sammy's wrinkles were like hieroglyphics, he said. She wore a long red robe and held out a single caramel on her flat palm, and Joe and his sisters ran screaming away.

I liked listening to Joe tell stories. That and the way he looked were basically why I was in love with the guy. I wished it hadn't been true, but that was one thing I never lied about. I was totally berserk about Joe.

Joe said he remembered the old Halloween smell of the wet pumpkin over his head as he waited for the caretaker on the front step. The old man came to the door, smoothing his hair like a married man. "Those nuns giving you trouble? Deer at your tomatoes?" he said. "Human hair, isn't that right, Sammy?" he called back into the dark house. "Only thing they're frightened of."

Joe left feeling scared as he had on Halloween, though he didn't run and he didn't scream but walked slowly to his car. I was getting impatient to hear about the nuns, and I asked Joe if he'd tell me more about the convent. Joe said one thing he really didn't like was to be rushed by a woman and I said, "Please forgive me for my sins." He said when he got back to the convent he went out to the pile of wet leaves where he threw the hair from the shower-house floor. I moved closer to him as he told me that the nuns had their hair cut once a month and it was his job to sweep up afterward. He said he wore his rubber boots as he swept all the spun orange hair and straight chestnut hair and twirls of black hair; he swept the waves and curls into a square of burlap, then threw the hair into the woods for the birds to make nests. The day he visited the old caretaker, he picked up a clump of hair and stuffed it into an old sock, which he tied to the stake of a tomato plant. He said a lot of tomatoes were saved.

"Do the nuns wear underwear when they shower?" I said.

I couldn't believe I'd said that. I'd always been totally embarrassed to take a shower after gym class; at every school I went to I always stuck my clothes right to my sweaty body. I couldn't believe it when Mary O'Brien danced around naked, screaming about Ricko, who worked at the gas station's loins.

"You have a pretty good shower in your house, great pressure," said Joe. And then he told me about when he was a little boy and took showers with his father, Julius Peretti. His father took the soap from his hairy chest and washed Joey's hair with his rough hands. Mr. Peretti liked to shower in the dark because he said real men took showers in the dark and he always talked of when he was a young boy, growing up in Naples. Every day in summer, Julius stood between his mother's legs as she sold dripping squares of hot pizza to all the tourists on their way home from sightseeing at Pompeii. Julius stood kicking the ground as his mother handed the cheese slabs to the dusty tourists. And whenever Julius tried to run off, his mother said if he wasn't careful hot cheese would drip down on his head.

I imagined standing naked in the shower with Joe and his father. God strike me down, I thought. "That's very interesting," I said to Joe. "What else did your father do?"

As soon as Julius was old enough to cook the pizzas himself, he ran away to America; there, in Boston, he married a girl from Naples. "They moved to Grove, where he opened a hardware store and played the horses and had three pretty daughters and one son, me," said Joe, pounding his fist on his chest.

I rolled down the window when we got to the Atlantic and breathed in the salty air. The sand was still wet as we walked along the shore. We kept bumping into each other as we walked over seaweed and dried-up crabs. At one point Joe put his hand on my arm. Dear God, I prayed, looking up at the gull-screaming sky, let him throw me down on the beach and make another Joey, Jr.

"Egrets," whispered Joe. Ahead of us was a flock of white birds. We both knelt down as Joe balanced the lens of his camera on my shoulder to take a close-up of one wounded bird with blood on a broken wing.

Guide me, O Lord, lead me in the paths of righteousness, I prayed. I stood up and ran ahead down the beach, hoping he would come running after me, but when I turned around, Joe had walked the other way.

On the drive home I sat a little closer to him and put my hand palm up between us on the seat, but he wouldn't look at me. He stared straight ahead, driving faster than he had before, telling story after story about growing up in Grove. He said he used to visit the butcher with his father once a week. The butcher took Joe and his father to a back room filled with raw pigs, hanging up around like a curtain. The butcher stood in his bloody white apron. " 'You see, Joey, I cut the animals in the night. I raise my knife and it shines in the moon. You see,' " — Joe lifted his hand from the steering wheel as he talked — " 'I bend my arm back to catch the moon. I bring it down and the moon slides into the meat.' " And then the butcher bent down and pinched Joe's cheek with his red fingers.

I wasn't listening; I was making calculations. He was twice my age. He smelled like burning leaves and his arms looked as if they were made by Michelangelo. I thought if my mother suspected anything she'd have the station wagon packed by sundown. It didn't quite work that way.

* * *

The morning after we went to the beach, Joe didn't drive the bus. A fat volunteer firewoman opened the door, and I thought maybe Joe had died in his sleep. He called right after I got home from school; Mrs. Flax answered the phone in the middle of making a batch of curried-egg canapés.

"Oh, hello, Mr. Caretaker. No, she's no sicker than she usually is."

Joe had come down with a bad case of the flu and was calling to see if I was all right. While Kate was swimming at the indoor pool at the high school, and Mrs. Flax was up to her elbows in eggs, I ran up to the convent. It was a sunny fall afternoon, and the nuns were kicking their way through the leaves. I snuck around the back paths, with one ear to the ground, one ear to the sky, but I heard nothing.

Joe's cottage was far back in the woods, stone and simple the way you'd think it would be. I knocked on the door, and when he didn't answer I crossed myself, then tiptoed in. There was one main room, with a fireplace and a kitchen table. There were photographs lined neatly on the wall, of all kinds of birds and an enlarged one of his sisters, arms flung around one another, mouths open, doing some kind of cancan with their legs kicking in the air. By the stove was a small framed picture of his mother; she wore a black dress and had big loose bosoms, and the picture was set up so it faced the jars of spices. In the center of the table was a cigar box full of postcards. I sorted through them as quietly as I could. They all were the same picture of the same palm tree and aqua sky, and they all said basically the same thing: "Visit soon. Palm tree in front yard!" They were signed "Flora," his middle sister.

I crept into the dark bedroom and sat in the rocking chair watching Joe sleep. He was breathing thickly under a web of blankets; his dark hair lay against a pillow like a flag, and he was wearing faded flannel pajamas and a V-neck sweater, backward. The clothes he usually wore, his corduroy pants, plaid shirt, and heavy jacket, were hanging on the wall. His moccasins, right and left, were waiting in the corner.

It was four o'clock and the nuns were in chapel. An old nun had rung the bell that day, the way she did on Joe's day off. I sat down on the edge of the bed and smelled violet perfume and tomato sauce. I wanted to kiss his forehead, and I sat very still, holding my hands tightly together to keep from touching him.

Joe moved his arm and opened his eyes. "Mom? Oh, hi, it's you. This is her sweater. You O.K.?"

I could feel his legs rubbing against my back.

Joe said a lot of the sisters were sick a few weeks before. The chapel was empty, the showers were empty, the whole place was more silent than usual. He had to go to the dormitory and bring food. They all seemed so sad, he said, lined up like little girls, sneezing and sneezing.

"D'you want me to tuck you in?" I said.

Joe shook his head and fell back to sleep. I could just see him helping his mother make tomato sauce, splitting the tomatoes, popping them out of their skins so the seeds filled his fingernails. He'd told me on the bus that his parents were married in November and so were all their friends. They sat around the kitchen table in our very same kitchen, playing cards, the women in their print dresses, the men in their undershirts, and in winter they often wore their coats inside. "Joey," his father would say and hit him on the head, "Joey, maybe some day you'll grow up and join the November club."

I knelt on the floor by Joe's bed and put my head on his feet, but all I could hear were the nuns laughing across the pond.

When I got home, Mrs. Flax was swinging furiously back and forth on the porch swing. As I climbed up the steps she said, "Where on earth have you been? Those boots have got to go. It's time you got some normal shoes."

Kate had come home from swim practice; she was sitting in the empty bathtub in her bathing suit, covered with green grease, ready to swim around the world.

4

M RS. FLAX drove down Main Street, waving her arms around and telling Kate and me how popular she'd been, growing up. I kept grabbing on to the steering wheel so we wouldn't crash, and she said if I did it one more time she'd let me out of the car.

Grove was a small town, Small Town, U.S.A., as they say, once a place where city people spent lazy summers, lying in hammocks on porches that wrapped around the wood houses. For years the town had been silent, but slowly the houses were being bought up again. As Mrs. Flax drove, I saw two men carrying a large mirror into a store, and I caught myself, my curly hair and haunted eyes, framed in the window of the station wagon.

Mrs. Flax drove to the old section of town, where all the buildings were fish-skin gray and the road was cracked from winter ice. She slowed the car outside Landsky's Shoe Store, with dusty shoes in the window and a dirty white awning overhead. We sat for a minute with the motor running while she put on a new shade of lipstick, "in the mauve family," Carrie had said. Mrs. Flax looked in the rear-view mirror and pinched her cheeks, and then she turned off the car. At the door of the store she pinched her cheeks again. I didn't want to be anything like her, I swear, but men always seemed to like her pink cheeks, so, God forgive me, I pinched mine until they hurt, then took Kate's hand and followed Mrs. Flax inside.

Mr. Landsky was a short man, with brown and gray hair and thick glasses. He got his first pair of glasses when he was four years old, and he had been president of his high school class years ago. He still lay in bed at night, making speeches. His brother did not complete school, and after he returned from the navy the brother opened his own shoe store, which he referred to as "the boutique," and changed his name to Land. His boutique was in the new part of town and was full of pointed, imported shoes, but Mrs. Flax took us to the regular shoe store, where Mr. Landsky sold shoes "with both their toe and their heel on the ground," as he said. Sneakers, play shoes, walking shoes, school shoes, and he always stocked the regulation black oxfords for the nuns at the convent. No matter if it wasn't his faith, he said. The sisters needed shoes, he gave them shoes.

When I saw the nun shoes on display, shiny black with skinny laces, I slid my hands deep inside. I shut my eyes and prayed. I wanted to be a nun. I wanted to sleep in a nun bed and I wanted to have a holy soul.

Mr. Landsky was friendly, welcoming us to town, asking us where we were from — a question that Kate always answered by raising her shoulders up to her ears and Mrs. Flax never answered.

"I'm from South Dakota, originally," said Mr. Landsky. "Can you imagine keeping kosher in South Dakota?" He leaned over and grabbed Kate's nose. "You know what we did if we used the wrong fork or the wrong spoon when I was a kid? We had to go out back and stick them in the ground, and when the ground was frozen solid that was not easy. We called it the Hardware Garden, can you believe it? The Hardware Garden?"

Mrs. Flax sat down in one of the leather chairs against the wall and took off one of her shoes. She sat there, examining the heel, pretending to be deaf, while Mr. Landsky talked Kate into maple-red shoes with a strap. Kate wanted to wear them right away, so he took her dirty sneakers and put them in the box.

I didn't want new shoes, though. I wasn't about to give up the one gift I'd received from my father. I told him I didn't need a new pair of shoes, thank you. He looked at Mrs. Flax for advice but she began humming "The Battle Hymn of the Republic," so he said, "Nice boots," and left me alone.

"I hope I see you at Parent/Teacher Night next week," said Mr. Landsky. He seemed to be talking to Mrs. Flax, but she just took off her other shoe.

I said thank you and asked if he had children, and he said they had all grown up and moved to the city.

While Mr. Landsky went back to the counter to write up a slip for Kate's shoes, the mother superior from the convent walked in, with a nun who didn't look old enough to order a drink if she wanted to. That was the first time I met Mother Superior. She was shaped like an Eskimo and looked like her black habit was sewn on. She looked at Kate's feet and said in her gentle voice, "What beautiful red shoes, dear," and she and the junior nun sat down next to Mrs. Flax.

Mr. Landsky put down his pen and walked from the back

of the store. "It's so nice to see you again, Reverend Mother," he said, and he took her plump hand. "We have nylon laces in black now. I think the sisters will like them."

I sat down next to the young nun. I wanted to ask her what color bra she was wearing and if she had pure thoughts every second of the day. I sat on my hands and pretended to stare at the cardboard cut-out display of Buster Brown and his cockeyed dog.

"Welcome to Grove," said Mother Superior, while Kate turned her ankles in and practiced walking on the sides of her new shoes.

When Mr. Landsky returned, he was balancing two boxes on one hand. There were drops of water on his white shirt, and his hair smelled of licorice as he sat on a stool in front of Mother Superior. He placed the boxes on the ground, then took two lollipops from his shirt pocket and handed them to Kate and me. I was totally embarrassed to be holding a lollipop in front of the nuns like that, so I handed mine to Kate.

Mother Superior crossed her leg and stretched it out so her foot was in Mr. Landsky's hand. He deftly unlaced one shoe and then the other, and I noticed there was green paint under his fingernails.

Mother Superior stood, placing one black-stockinged foot on the metal ruler, and Mr. Landsky held her calf with both hands.

"Most women's feet get bigger, but you're still a perfect seven," he said.

"That's when they get married," muttered Mrs. Flax. "Their feet swell."

Mr. Landsky took a black shoe from the top box and a shoehorn from his back pocket. He placed the shoehorn behind Mother Superior's heel as she slipped into the new shoe. Mr. Landsky tied the new oxfords, gave them a little pat, then flipped her old shoes into the box.

"We only need one more pair now," said Mother Superior, looking at the young, silent nun. "Fewer each year."

Before we left, Mr. Landsky handed Kate a bumper sticker with RENAISSANCE IN GROVE printed in red, white, and blue. As soon as we got outside, Mrs. Flax whispered, "That chief nun had crumbs on her robe."

"She's a holy vessel," I said.

"Will you guys try and act like human beans," said Kate, sticking the bumper sticker on the bottom of one new shoe.

As we drove away, I knelt in the back seat, watching the nun car driving slowly behind us.

"That Mr. Landsky has good hands," sighed Mrs. Flax.

The black nun car moved behind us like a boat as it drifted slowly around the curves of the road. We left them farther and farther behind, but I could see that when yellow leaves fell on their windshield, Mother Superior turned on the wipers to brush them away, and I vowed at that moment to ask her, as soon as I found the courage, how to hear the Word of God.

5

I STOPPED taking the bus to school because I wanted to purge every sinful thought about Joe Poseidon Peretti from my soul. So twice a day I did plodding penance in my vinyl boots. I got a job at Landsky's Shoe Store afternoons to earn money for a pilgrimage to somewhere, and I checked every pair of shoes that walked in the place to see if they belonged to my father. Mostly I listened to Lou Landsky drone on about the renaissance in Grove and how his grandfather brought a goat to shul every morning of his bearded life in Russia.

The best part of the job was when Mr. Landsky was not around. Then I turned the OPEN sign to CLOSED and lay down on a pile of broken shoes behind the counter, smelling the leather and trying to remember my father. Once I found a broken-down pair of nun shoes and I put them up to my ears like shells to hear the Sacred Word, but all I heard was some delirious mother pounding on the front door, desperate to buy her kids saddle shoes.

Mrs. Flax seemed to like Grove at first, and as long as she liked a place we stayed. She even said she wouldn't get sick if she went to Parent/Teacher Night at my school and invited Kate and me along for the ride.

Mr. Crain, my history teacher, stood at the door to the classroom, grinning at the parents and students, pretending he was running for governor, calling everybody by name in every single sentence he said.

"I think he's one of the original Pilgrims," muttered Mrs. Flax as she sashayed in.

The classroom was full of parents standing around their kids' desks and kids trying to pretend they didn't have parents. In the corner was Lou Landsky, looking messier than I'd ever seen him look, with orange paint in his hair. That was the night I found out that along with wanting to be a second baseman, Lou was a Sunday and evening painter.

Mrs. Flax marched right over to him, and I took Kate to stand next to the table with the pale blue globe of the world. We watched Lou get Mrs. Flax a Dixie cup of wine from on top of Mr. Crain's desk. They stood holding the little cups in both hands, and Mrs. Flax burst out laughing with her face up in the air. I began to spin the globe like a crazy woman when Lou turned in his paint-splattered shoes like a child and actually spilled his drink on the classroom floor. All the parents and their sons and daughters saw what was going on. When Mr. Crain knocked his knuckles on the blackboard for everyone to quiet down, not one person shut up, and while he gave his speech called "Community Begins in the Classroom," we were all watching Mrs. Flax and Lou become an item.

The morning after Parent/Teacher Night, we found a bouquet of autumn leaves on the porch swing and a note for Mrs. Flax from Lou. Lou said he usually didn't talk to

women when the World Series was on, but it wasn't long
before she was going on sleep-over dates.

One day in early November, Mrs. Flax informed me she
was leaving town for one night. She wasn't going with Lou.
I never found out where she went, maybe to visit my father,
but she said Kate would spend the night with some other
little girl and she didn't want me to stay alone. Mary
O'Brien's mother didn't let her have sleep-over friends because there were already eight kids in the house, so Mrs.
Flax had the bright idea of having me sleep over at her
boyfriend's, my boss Lou's.

Lou lived alone in a three-story house, and I arrived there
on Friday evening after closing up the store. When I
walked into Lou's kitchen, he was banging around, hitting
a paintbrush against his thigh. While I still had my overnight bag in my hand, he said, "You know, I'm married,
I'm still legally married. I was up on the goddamn third floor
in my studio and my Sophia was in the middle of vacuuming, when she puts down the handle, doesn't even turn the
damn thing off, and walks out of the house and never
comes back."

Lou smacked the paintbrush against the refrigerator. I
put down my bag and surveyed the kitchen while Lou continued to rant about his Sophia. There were oil paintings
stacked everywhere — on the table and chairs, all over
the counters, on top of the refrigerator, everywhere but
the walls — and there were gobs of paint stuck to the
floor.

That night I went to sleep in the canary yellow room
with butterflies painted all over the walls. In the middle of
the night it began to thunder and lightning. Once a baby-

sitter in Alabama told me that if you wear sneakers you'll always be grounded, so I got up and found an old pair of sneakers in the closet. Who knows, they could have been Sophia's. I couldn't get back to sleep, though, so I staggered into the kitchen and found Lou sitting at the table. He was wearing a red-and-white striped bathrobe, and he was forking coffee ice cream out of a carton into his mouth. A small glass of red wine was balanced on his thigh.

"Get a fork and pull up a chair," he said.

I took a painting of *Sophia as Toreador* off a chair and sat down next to him. He handed me a fork, saying, "You know the best thing I did as a kid was watch sandlot ball on the sabbath. There was nothing in the Talmud against baseball. Of course, we walked there, couldn't take the bus, couldn't listen to the radio. Here," he said, handing me the carton of ice cream. "You should grow up to be free. Do you understand me? Free," he said, poking his fork at my shoulder.

I was getting very tired.

"Do you know what my mother used to say to me?" he said, leaning forward, spilling the glass of wine down into the cuff of his pants. "She'd say, 'Lou, you're like a boarder in the house. You're a lazy boy, just like a boarder in the house.' "

He kept talking until I thought I was going to fall off my chair. As I walked out of the kitchen, the thunder crashed and I heard him say, "*Ah fluch zu Columbus*, a curse on Columbus."

I went to sleep with the sneakers on and was not struck by lightning. I thought if I was more daring, God would send me a message, but lightning on my feet was not the way I really wanted to hear the Word.

The next morning I wandered around the house, pretending I knew what I was doing, and bumped into Lou in the bathroom, shaving in his underwear. The first man I saw in his underwear was a sleep-over guest of Mrs. Flax's, either in Arkansas or Louisiana — I always confuse the two. The guy didn't say boo to me, but when I stood on the toilet and asked if I could shave, too — I must have been four years old — he patiently dabbed shaving cream on my face, took the blade out of the razor, and let me shave clean. When I was done, he wiped the shaving cream out of my ears and we smiled at each other in the steamy mirror.

For breakfast Lou took me up to his attic studio, with round windows and jars of pencils and crayons and tall cans of soft brushes. He set down two bowls of cereal and blueberries for us, blueberries his Sophia had frozen for him before she ran away. For a moment I wanted to pat Lou's head and say I was sorry he had kids who didn't visit and a runaway wife and he wasn't a second baseman in spring and summer and a full-time painter the rest of the year.

By the time Mrs. Flax came to pick me up the cereal milk had turned light blue, and she ran right to Lou and hooped her arms around his neck. The first time I saw her kiss a man was in the summer, near a sandy beach. She was wearing a white bathing suit and the man had on a faded madras bathing suit and they were kissing, leaning against a peeling wood-paneled station wagon. I remember thinking that I was the adult and she was my child. I tried to remember ever being inside her, but I couldn't imagine she'd let me hang around for nine months in a row.

That night there was a swim meet at school, Kate's first one in Grove. On the way to the school I sat in back, massaging her feet the way I always did before a race, as she began to explain her goldfish theory of the universe. Basically her notion was that goldfish grow to whatever size container they are in. If they lived in the ocean you could get a goldfish the size of an orange whale. If you put the goldfish in a teacup that's about all you got. We never argued with Kate about fish. It was something she was extremely stubborn about. When she was still waddling, Mrs. Flax gave her a few fish in a fishbowl from the five-and-dime. Kate was furious and threw a baby temper tantrum. Then she got silent and took an envelope from Mrs. Flax's desk. She scooped the fish out of the bowl with a spoon and dumped them in the envelope, then waddled out of the house and threw the envelope in the blue mailbox on the corner. She came back banging the spoon on her head, saying something about sending the fish back to the ocean where they belonged.

We got to the school and walked across the gymnasium floor, which was polished like a candied apple. We paraded through to the chlorine-drenched swimming pool. Benches were lined up on either side, one side full of families from Grove, the other with the team and fans of the neighboring town. Kate pulled off her clothes and ran in her turquoise bathing suit to stand next to a bunch of kids and her coach, who was built like Santa Claus, in her red sweat outfit. The kids from Grove looked like refugees in all their different-colored bathing suits, shivering and wiggling around. The kids from the next town were sitting in an even line on one of the benches, all with navy blue sweat shirts with orange stripes down the sides. When their coach blew a whistle, they all stood and took off their sweat clothes and they all were wearing identical orange and blue swim suits.

Mrs. Flax and I sat down next to Mr. Landsky, who leaned over and pointed to a card table full of snacks across the pool. "Coca-Cola," he said, "who would believe it. In Russia they didn't drink Coke. They sat around drinking tea out of tall glasses. And they let these kids drink Cokes after they swim. Who would believe it?"

But Mrs. Flax wasn't listening and I wasn't listening, because as Lou began some story about how his grandmother used to make *shettles* — "You know, wigs, and I'd tease her, just joking, that there was a hair in the soup" — Joe, Joe Poseidon, appeared in the doorway, wearing his beaded moccasins, an old pair of corduroy pants, and a forest green sweater. Mrs. Flax began swinging her leg back and forth and I slid down the bench away from her, toward Joe.

"Hello there, Mr. Joseph Peretti, why don't you come sit down?" hissed Mrs. Flax, but a whistle blew for the races and everyone quieted down. Joe quickly ducked past both of us and sat far away as the moon.

Everyone turned toward the swimmers, while Kate stood with her red hair curling out of her cap and her toes curling over the edge of the pool. Her arms were back like angel wings. The whistle blew and the racers dove into the air, then smacked onto the water. Watching Kate swim was magic. Mothers from both towns, big, chalky women, held bags of cookies and stood right at the edge of the pool, screaming at their blue-lipped children to win. The neighboring town had better swimmers as a group, but Kate won every race she entered, the breast stroke, the butterfly, and the crawl.

"You shudda had a faster time, you know I worked with you on that. Breathe quicker, you have to breathe quicker," screamed one mother as her daughter hung on the side of the pool, spitting up water.

When the last race was over, Kate pulled herself out of the pool and walked dripping over to us. I handed her a towel, which she put around her shoulders, but she didn't say a word. She just stood shivering in a puddle, pulling a thread of towel with her teeth, while Lou went on about how she was a red-headed Esther Williams.

Kate said, "C'mon, fans, let's get out of here."

The other kids were hanging around having Cokes and cookies with their mothers, but Kate never believed in that. I would have sold my soul to have Joe look at me, but Kate was dragging us out like she'd robbed the place, so I just grabbed her trophies and left.

On the way from the school to the supermarket, I sat in back with Kate and rubbed her feet, praying that I'd have a vision at the check-out counter. Mrs. Flax sped around the corners, as I pleaded with her to at least use her blinker.

Supermarkets in the free world had different meanings for each of us. Mrs. Flax was as dangerous in the aisles as she was on the road, flying by the shelves, throwing the ingredients for her latest puffs and canapés into the cart. Kate often was mesmerized by the tuna fish and stood staring forlornly up at the stacks of cans. I personally kept an eye out for the strange bread Ezekiel snacked on or a family-size package of locusts and wild honey as I headed toward the fresh fruit. There I squinted my eyes to see a halo around me in the mirror above the apples and oranges. But that afternoon in Grove, Mrs. Flax was calling us from the front of the store before holy light had time to pour through my soul. I took some apples, found Kate, and joined Mrs. Flax, who was cracking peanuts in her teeth so they popped open and crumbled all down her coat. "Don't forget these," she said, holding up a handful of shells to the check-out girl. I looked to the heavens as the girl slowly pulled each apple toward her, trying not to chip her fingernails.

When we got in the house Mrs. Flax didn't empty the

bag. She just went into her room and slammed the door, while I washed the apples and put the rest of the food away. Then Kate and I went into our room, where I lined up Kate's new trophies and she spread out her rock collection on the floor, the way she did after every swim meet. There were rocks all over the floor when the doorbell rang.

"She can get it," I said, pretending it was somebody selling something, maybe a guy selling Jehovah's Witness magazines, even though we could hear Lou's laughing voice.

I sat down on my bed and began to rock the way little kids do in their playpens, rocking, rocking. Kate used to do it when she was a baby, and I began to sing, "Old Mac-Donald had a farm, ee eye ee eye o."

Kate said, "Stop it," but I couldn't stop and kept singing and rocking back and forth. "Old Macdonald Had a Farm" and the "ee eye ee eye o" bit made me think of going blind, which I was always scared of and I thought of Helen Keller, who scared me even more.

Finally we heard a car running, and Kate stood up and looked out the window. "I guess she's going out on a date," she said. "I guess she's sewing her wild goats."

I stopped singing, just kept rocking, and then I lay down on the bed. When I kicked the wall hard with my boot, Kate said, "Stop kicking the wall will you? Who do you think you are, Miss Teenager of the World?"

As I kicked the wall late into the night, I decided to starve myself to have a vision.

6

⚭

$\mathbf{M}$Y FAST lasted exactly two meals and then I was just a regular girl.

We were studying American history in school, and one gray day, while Mr. Crain stood at the blackboard, shuffling baseball cards, about to choose two students to prepare an imaginary debate between Louis XIV and Franklin Delano Roosevelt, Mrs. Crain, his wife, poked her crew-cut head in the door. I thought she was going to make some announcement about giving a special test for the problem kids in the class or embarrass her husband and the rest of us by bringing a banana-smelling bag of lunch he'd forgotten at home, but Mrs. Crain went right up to her husband and they stood whispering against the chalky blackboard like they were in their own garage. Mrs. Crain put her hand up so it almost touched Mr. Crain's ear, and she whispered in a whisper that the whole class could hear. "The president has been shot," she said. "The president is dead."

Mr. Crain dropped the baseball cards. I watched them flutter to the floor, then lifted the dittoed chart of checks and balances to my face, breathing in the purple ink. A hoody boy in the back row took out a scratchy transistor radio. As we sat listening to the news, I peeled a bumper sticker with the president's name off my loose-leaf binder.

School closed early and I ran all the way home, holding my breath for as long as I could and crossing myself over my coat. Mrs. Flax and Kate were already there, and we sat down in a row on the couch and watched the television. But I couldn't sit. After a few minutes I stood up and switched the channels, clicking around to every station, wanting to see something different; but on every channel, all over the country, everyone was crying, except me.

"Stop that and sit down," said Mrs. Flax. "It's not natural for you not to cry. Our president has been shot. For God's sake, will you cry?" But I wouldn't shed a tear. I could feel tears trying to climb up the backs of my knees, but my face was dry as paper.

Kate was crying in child gulps, and when her dress was completely wet with tears she jumped off the couch and ran into the bathroom. She turned on the water full blast and spent the rest of the day sitting in the tub. While I was standing in front of the television set, Carrie knocked at the door with her plastic cosmetics case full of the newest sample lipsticks and candy perfumes.

I answered the door, and Carrie said, "Hi, honey, it's a sad day, a very sad day. He had such beautiful hair."

Mrs. Flax called from the couch that she didn't think this was an ideal day for make-up, but Carrie planted herself at the door and gave a talk on how everyone, especially Catholics, had to look their best on a day like this.

I opened the door wide and welcomed her inside. I stood

behind them as they sat on the couch, watching film clips of the president's life. There he was, standing on a battleship, playing football by the sea, sitting at his desk with a pen in his hand, and holding his daughter on his shoulders.

"Such beautiful hair," said Carrie.

Kate sounded like she was wrestling with an octopus in the bathtub, and Mrs. Flax asked me to check if she was all right.

I bowed to her behind her back, then walked by the bathroom and waved to Kate. She waved back and I snuck into Mrs. Flax's room and fell down on the knobby white bedspread. It felt like there were no adults left on the whole planet. I lay with my face down, the bedspread tattooing my face, praying to God to explain what the meaning of his act was. I didn't lose my faith then, but I did begin on that day to think that maybe the job was too big for one deity. I flipped over and stared up at the light on the ceiling, which was full of dead moth shadows.

I felt tears right behind my eyes, ready to come screaming out, and I had to slap my face to keep from crying. It was time to go to the convent.

As I walked through the living room, hugging myself, Carrie said, "You've got the eyes, honey, but remember the eyes are just the frosting on the cake."

I pushed open the door and walked like a robot onto the porch. What did truly holy people do? is what I wanted to know. I spit at the bare November trees. Inside, Mrs. Flax and Carrie were watching the crowds on TV, in Missouri and Maine, everywhere, crying like the next Ice Age had come.

As I staggered up the hill I wondered if my father was watching television, the same television stations as everyone else in the world. Maybe he was on the floor of a straw hut in the jungles of Brazil and he didn't even know what had happened. Maybe he was kissing his Brazilian wife's fingers and his Brazilian children's toes like it was a regular day.

The hedges on either side of the road were stale brown, and I decided if I could find one person who was not crying, I would be able to bear the pain. At the top of the hill I stood holding the cold bars of the convent gate, waiting to see a dry-eyed nun, but the first nun I saw was an old woman, thin as a stick, crying into her prayer book, the tears staining the pages as she walked. The old woman passed, and I stood in a cloud of incense from her heavy black robes.

I pinched my cheeks, then ran to the bell tower, racing up the steep steps to see Joe.

He was sitting hunched on the bench, looking blankly out at the dark pond. We nodded to each other and as soon as I sat down he began to sniffle like a child. I looked out across the convent grounds. The world had stopped. The paths winding through the woods looked like they'd been there since dinosaurs stalked the earth.

"The white man has lost his mind," said Joe. "This never would have happened with the tribal councils."

He stood and began to pull the bell rope, stopping the bell each time with his hands, the way the old caretaker had shown him, for "when a person takes his last do-si-do." The bell rang out over the convent, bellowing across the pond until I thought my unholy life would pour out of my eyes and the nuns would have to jump on Noah's ark to survive.

"I think I should be getting back," I said, standing up.

Joe began telling me about the old caretaker who'd had the job before. The wrinkled man had limped around with his cane as he'd given Joe a tour, grabbing him by the elbow and steering him around the convent grounds. It was a fast tour, under the willows that circled the pond, then back to the tower at the gate. As they climbed the steps Joe thought the frail man would fall back into his arms, but they both made it to the top. The old man stood panting. "So," he said, "you Catholic? You have a holy soul? It's a good job, you work hard, but my legs are gone." And he hit Joe's legs with his cane. "You can see everything from up here, just like Him up there." The old man held the cane above his head. "And that pond water is colder than ice."

Joe said the old man had Indian ways, the way he could stand so quiet with his heels together like a little dancer. Before he handed Joe the keys to the convent, he pointed his cane across the pond at Mother Superior's cottage and said, "She's keeping a secret. Most people are."

When I asked Joe what the secret was, he said, "Maybe you shouldn't come up here."

I took his advice and solemnly walked down the steps. I didn't leave, though. I sat in the stairwell with the stone pressing cold on my legs. I locked my arms around my knees and prayed Joe would come flying down to save me. Whenever Kate got lonely, wherever we were, I promised to find a sheep and hollow it out so we could nestle warm inside. But there were no sheep in sight. I tiptoed back up the steps and stood shivering right behind Joe. He had his head in his hands and his shoulders shook with sobs as the sun dropped into the pond.

I sat down next to him, held my breath, and put my arm around his broad back. He turned to me and put his arms lightly on my shoulders. We sat on the cold bench that way, shivering from the cold and from fear, and then we kissed.

Our lips bumped up against each other as we tried to line them up. We didn't open our mouths. It was several minutes of soft kisses on the lips. O Lord, I prayed, mea culpa, mea culpa. And then we kissed some more.

"Joseph! Joseph!" Mother Superior's voice boomed out across the pond, just as I was running out of air, and I jumped up and bolted down the stairs.

At home I sat out on the porch swing, hugging myself, swinging back and forth in the wind. The chains from the swing squeaked as the bell began to ring again from the tower. I was scared I had a baby growing inside me already, a baby standing up and dancing around. I know it's crazy, but I thought maybe we'd made the new Indian-Italian-Jewish messiah, and I vowed not to tell even Mary O'Brien what we had done.

When the bell stopped ringing I went inside. As I opened the refrigerator and stared at the chocolate-cookie and whipped-cream cake I had made for Kate, Mrs. Flax called from her room, "Where on earth have you been, young lady? If you go up to that convent again we'll have to move!"

I stood stuffing the cake in my mouth, apologizing to God for not being able to starve myself, then tiptoed down the hall. I stood in the dark at Kate's bunk, listening to her breathe. I kissed her forehead and smelled her chlorine curls and prayed we wouldn't move. Carrie said Kate had her own personal "eau de cologne." When I mentioned it to Kate, she told me, "Mind your own bee's wax. Who do you want me to smell like, Thomas Jefferson?"

I lay down on my bed, put my hands on my stomach, and prayed there wasn't a Joey, Jr., beneath my fingertips. "All right, Lord," I prayed, "I've been as bad as I can be. Now it's your move. Now I want to be saved."

7

THE NEXT MORNING I got up when there was still frost on the ground. I walked into town, trying to see if people could tell I was a fallen woman, but not one horn honked and no cars stopped. When I got to the village square I stopped and stared at the flag, whipping itself at half-mast in the wind. The whole world was moping about the president, and I wanted to be burned at the stake.

I walked over to Landsky's and stared at my reflection in the dirty window, surrounded by dozens of shoes. "Well, kids, I'm a sex kitten, can you tell?" I whispered.

The door was locked, but I could see Lou in the back, with his hand in a high heel, slowly polishing it creamy white. I knocked on the door, and he came to let me in with his free hand, holding the one in the shoe above his head. He didn't seem to notice I'd turned into a woman overnight. He went back to his polishing, dripping small drops of white on the floor, and began to talk about the way Grove used to be, when the neighborhood boys came over and played running bases on warm spring nights. They always wore their pajamas, he said, when Mr. Crain and Joe Peretti were kids, and I said an inner prayer for Joe's pajamas. Lou said he couldn't believe that children could one day be oiling their mitts and throwing sneakers over telephone wires and before you could snap your fingers they cared about women and countries and killing a man. Mr. Landsky held the white shoe over his heart.

I missed the president and I missed my father and I wanted to confess my kiss to them both.

I spent the morning at the store, trying to calm myself by practicing tacking heels on an old pair of bowling shoes, as Lou talked about growing up in South Dakota.

"Things were different in my kid days," he said. "You know what my mother used to say? *'Ah fluch zu Columbus'* —a curse on Columbus. That's when the trouble began."

When I got home everyone was still crying on TV and Kate was on the floor with her rocks. I sat with my hand on the phone in the kitchen, waiting for Joe to come by and propose, but there was no word from him or heaven above.

At six o'clock that evening I decided to purify my soul and asked Kate if she wanted to go for a swim. Within two minutes she was in the car, wearing her bathing suit under her clothes and her bathing cap on her head. Coach had given her the key to the pool at school, to use whenever she had the urge.

I looked at myself in the mirror to see if I looked more mature, most sophisticated, more like a love goddess, more like a sinner, and Kate said, "Who do you think is following us, the Mafia?"

I put one hand on my knee and tried to feel if my knee felt different or my hand felt different, and I wanted to have a brief conversation with Joan of Arc.

The parking lot was empty and I drove straight around

back to the gymnasium. The place was pitch dark, and I put my hand on Kate's bathing-capped head as she guided me back to the pool.

"Swim!" she shouted into the dark, and it echoed back, "Swim, swim!"

"Kate!" I shouted as I heard her dive in. "Kate, my child, are you there?"

I pressed myself to the wall and crept along until I felt the light switches and flicked them on, then pulled off my clothes. I hadn't been swimming since Kate was born. No saint had ever been beatified in chlorine, as far as I knew, and I'd given it up as a frivolous pleasure. I dove in naked, feeling the water pour cool over my skin, and raced back and forth with Kate. I was winded after four laps and dove down deep to the bottom of the pool and put my fingers to my lips where Joe had kissed me.

I came up for breath, swam to the side, and dunked my hair back at the edge of the pool. I pulled myself out and stood naked, with my arms straight out to the sides. "Take me, Joe, and take me, Lord," I whispered up to the fluorescent lights.

Kate poked his head up, treading water. "Whadd'ya think this is, Las Vegas?" she yelled, and then went back to her laps.

When the heavy door pushed open, I was putting on my dress. I quickly buttoned myself up as Lou walked in with a towel around his shoulders, carrying his paint-splattered shoes.

"Hi, Charlotte. Your mother said I'd find you two here. The man was a true liberal and the C.I.A. wanted a new man up at bat," he said, unzipping his pants. I looked away but he was wearing his bathing suit underneath. His hairy chest was also splattered with paint. He rolled his clothes into a ball and threw them to me to hold. I could smell Mrs. Flax's "Occur" perfume in his pants.

"You know what it makes me want to do?" he said. "Makes me want to cry into my goddamn baseball glove." Lou belly-flopped into the pool, splashing water all over me. He did one sloppy lap and hung on to the far side, while Kate continued to swim back and forth, in perfect form, racing along the black eel stripes.

"You going in?" Lou asked as he tried to hoist himself out of the pool. "Your mother said you could stop by if you want." He grunted as he finally pulled himself out. He walked over to me and I handed him his clothes, trying not to touch his wet hand.

"My Sophia left a cake in the freezer before she left, and I suppose today's the day to take it out," he said, stepping his wet legs into his pants.

I wondered if he could tell if I was a tainted woman. Maybe the whole town was going to have a holiday. Traffic would be blocked off. I'd ride on a float made of red crepe paper and sit waving with a toothy smile.

I knelt at the end of the pool, and when Kate came slithering up to do a flip turn I tapped her on the shoulder.

At Lou's house we took stacks of paintings off the chairs in the kitchen and sat with towels wrapped around our wet heads. Lou interrogated us as we gulped down partially defrosted pieces of carrot cake and ginger ale.

"So," he said, "what's to become of all this swimming?"

"Don't know," said Kate, eating the cake with her water-wrinkled fingers.

"She's Olympic material," I said.

"D'you have a boyfriend, Charlotte?"

"No, why? No!" I choked on my ginger ale.

"So, that pretty mother of yours keeps saying she's going to leave Grove," Lou said, leaning back in his chair. "You girls think she will?"

I put down my glass. "We should get home now. Kate's in training."

"Here, take a piece for your mother."

"She doesn't like cake," I said, and we stood up to leave.

Driving home I let Kate sit on my lap and steer for a while.

"He likes Mom a lot," she said. "Boys like her."

"He's not a boy. He's a man," I said, clicking my fingernails against the steering wheel and praying I wasn't pregnant.

8

I THINK God put the following days on slow motion. Thanksgiving Day arrived, and still Joe had not shot an arrow with a note into the tree outside my window. The man had not even telephoned.

I woke up early that morning to find snow pressed white against the windows. A blizzard had crept up on Grove, coating the hills and freezing the whole town. Lou even leaned an old brown-tinted photograph of the last big blizzard against a pair of golf shoes in the window display, with people sliding on wide wood skis down the middle of Main Street. It would be the coldest winter since the Revolutionary War, was what people were saying in Grove.

Mrs. Flax didn't believe in celebrating holidays, and I said I'd have a heart attack if she gave us hors d'oeuvres for a Thanksgiving meal, so I cooked a turkey and made a fairly convincing pumpkin pie. Kate spent the day in the bathtub, wearing a green paper Indian headband she'd made in school.

"Thank God they didn't make the child wear one of those Pilgrim hats," said Mrs. Flax.

I was in the kitchen, trying to set the table as serenely as possible, using one of Kate's trophies as a centerpiece, when the telephone rang. I was scared it would not be Joe and I couldn't bear to say hello to one of Mrs. Flax's gentleman callers, so I let it ring.

"Charlotte," Mrs. Flax called from her room. "Do you notice a very annoying sound?"

I washed my hands and slowly wiped them on a towel. Then I turned on the light in the oven and waved to the turkey, and finally I answered the phone.

"Hello? Oh, hi," I whispered, crossing myself with my free hand. "Sledding? Sure." I didn't want to say Joe's name out loud. "Yes, thank you, thank you, thank you very much."

"Who is it?" Mrs. Flax was calling from her room. "Who is on the phone?"

"Nobody," I said as I hung up.

"Charlotte Flax. I'm warning you," she said, "that man is too old for you."

The roads were plowed that afternoon, and after our meal Joe came by. I ran through the snow to the car and sat as close as possible without actually sitting on the man's lap.

All he would say was, "The Indians used to eat *wasna.* That's buffalo meat mashed with berries." And then we sat silently peering through the frosted glass. I waited for him to talk about our sacred kiss and how he wanted to drive north with me and live in an igloo forever, but his lips didn't move.

We rounded a slippery corner, almost setting up permanent residence in a snow drift, and Joe turned off the car. Then he said something softly. I leaned toward him to hear his words of love, but I didn't understand what he said.

I nodded as he lifted his sled from the back seat. He

dropped the sled in the snow and I trudged after him up the hill, my hands stuck, freezing, in the pockets of my coat.

We reached the top of the hill and stood staring down on the smooth, white fields. There were bird tracks and a scatter of pine cones, but other than that the snow was blank. I stood holding my coat collar tight around my neck as the wind slid down my back. Joe dove on the sled and flew straight down the hill, getting smaller and smaller, his black hair flying against the snow.

I screamed down at him, although I knew he couldn't hear. "Why don't you love me, Joe? Why don't you come back up here and love me forever?"

I tried not to love him. I knew that would be simpler. I thought if I could figure out why I did love him so much then I could make that sick feeling go away. I loved him because he had the most beautiful olive skin in captivity and I loved him because he wore his moccasins even though his feet must have been like blocks of ice.

I decided if he never came back I would stand on top of the hill for eternity, frozen in the snow, a scarecrow saint with icicles growing from her fingers.

When Joe came back up I grabbed the sled and fell on my stomach, pushing off down the hill. I tried to follow in his tracks but I couldn't steer with my cold hands. I raced faster and faster until I flew off the sled, landing in the snow as the sled raced past me, slicing past my red hands. I lay face down in the snow and smelled birthday candles burning down in the frosting of a long-ago cake at someone else's party. I remember the mother of the birthday girl opening the door and throwing the burning candles out into the snow. All the little girls ran to the window to watch the flames blow out in the wind.

I prayed we could be the characters in *Ethan Frome*. Joe and I could crash together on the sled and we would end up living together, broken but together. But Joe only wanted solo rides.

I stood up and hit the snow off me, and as the snow flurried in front of my eyes I saw a winter mirage. I saw the nuns ice-skating, figure-eighting gracefully in their black robes, the blades sparkling up under their habits. While Joe was taking one last run, I hugged the nearest pine tree, rubbing my face against the cold, rough bark, my arms not reaching all around. Joe once told me that the trees were his ancestors, and I imagined I was hugging the first Joe Peretti to walk the earth.

"Where in the world have you been?" Mrs. Flax shouted into my ear as soon as I got home. "I can only stay in one place so long."

I turned on the stove to warm my hands and said, "Oh, Christ."

"Some nun you'd make," she said, and I stalked into my room.

Kate was sitting on the top bunk, reading a large library book called *Fish Are Our Friends*.

"Do you know they don't even know how long some fish are?" she said, leaning over the bunk. "People only see 'em under water. They're optical confusions."

I lay down and kicked the wall. I know it doesn't make my IQ look too high, but I was sure I had Joe's child growing inside me.

9

※

THE MORE Joe ignored me the more nervous I got, and as I sat at my desk at school I was sure I could feel something kick. There was a Planned Parenthood office in the next town. I'd heard girls talking about it, whispering into their open lockers, so one day I skipped school and made my frightened journey.

Mrs. Flax had been getting rides to work with a nice young man from the office, so I took the car, driving slowly along the icy roads, peering through the steering wheel. I decided that if the doctor said I was pregnant I'd tell him there'd been virgin births before.

I parked the car outside a small yellow house. There was a wooden sign in the middle of the snowy lawn, listing Planned Parenthood, a dentist, and a chiropractor.

I tried to look as old as I could as I entered the crowded waiting room. The way I did this was to not blink, so I walked in there like a zombie. I sat on a hard plastic chair among a cluster of teenage girls and one pregnant woman trying to balance a screaming baby on her big lap. There was one boy, one greasy teenage boy, who was crouching on the floor next to his girlfriend's chair, pretending to read a little pamphlet on birth control. Two girls from Catholic school sat on a chair together, whispering in their plaid uniforms.

"Just tell the doctor you're a virgin if he asks," said one.

"I *am* a virgin," whispered the other.

"I know, I know, but don't let him think you'd ever really need this stuff."

I held my stomach and for a moment I thought I was going to give birth right there on the plastic chair, but finally the nurse, a young woman with thick ankles, called out Joan Ark, the name I had given, in a voice that sounded to me like a scream.

In the examining room, I lay on my back in a white paper robe and looked out the window at the snow falling on the street. I tried to relax by chanting the names on the green tubes of paint in Lou's studio: Sap Green, Viridian Green. Then I thought of the baseball player Pumpsie Green. I could hear the metallic sound of someone being weighed in the next room.

The doctor, fifty and well fed, walked in.

"Hello," he said as he pulled on a plastic glove. "I'm Doctor Reynolds," and he scooped his finger inside me. The nurse with thick ankles stood by.

"How do you do?" I said.

"How's school?" asked Doctor Reynolds, wiggling his finger.

"It's great. I wish we had school on weekends."

"How old are you, Joan?"

"What? Eighteen. Is anything inside me? I mean, is everything O.K.?"

Dr. Reynolds pulled out his hand, stripped off the glove,

and looked away, saying, "Come into my office as soon as you're dressed."

I got dressed and sat alone in Dr. Reynolds's mustard and green office and waited. I tried to focus on the color photographs of his children and the old map of America on the wall, but I couldn't focus. I couldn't wait any longer, so I jumped up and darted out of his office. As I ran for my coat in the waiting room, I noticed one of the pamphlets with a picture of a smiling pregnant woman on the front. The woman's hands were clasped around her big belly and the caption read: "I Am a Woman Giving Birth to Myself," and I thought it was quite possible I had not yet been born.

Out in the parking lot I lay on my back on the hood of the car, my arms straight out, and I opened my mouth to the falling snow.

A few days later, after listening to the girls at their lockers talking about Aunt Sammy the witch woman, who gave out birth control, I decided I should be prepared if Joe was ever in the mood to touch the vessel called my body again.

Two days later I didn't go home right after school. Instead, I walked downtown to Aunt Sammy's house behind the railroad station. There were boards missing on the porch, like lost teeth, so I stood nervously straddling two planks as I knocked on the door. I turned to leave the moment I knocked, but a second later a woman with white fluffy hair, wearing sequined sunglasses, opened the door. She was wearing a Hawaiian flowered shirt, red stretch pants, and red patent leather shoes.

"Come in, dear, it's one dollar," said Aunt Sammy, and she held out her arm, palm up, like an Egyptian painting.

I handed her all the change I had and walked in. Everything in the house was red. The carpet was red, the chairs were red, the curtains were red, and there were hundreds of curled photographs on the wall, all of them crooked, all of babies.

"Now, you *want* to be pregnant, or you want to *get* pregnant, or you *don't* want to be pregnant, or you *don't* want to get pregnant. It's always one of the four."

I opened my mouth and I have no idea what I was going to say, but Aunt Sammy said, "My toast is burning. I'm just making some eggs."

Aunt Sammy hurried into the kitchen, and I thought about leaving, but the red and the babies were comforting in a peculiar sort of way. Aunt Sammy returned with a plate of wet scrambled eggs.

"Here," she said, and I tried to balance the plate on my knees. I took a small forkful to be polite, but they had a distinct taste of being cooked in a washing machine.

"The toast!" Aunt Sammy gasped, and I followed her into the kitchen.

I had thought we were alone, but there was an old man, gnarled as a carrot, seated at the table, calmly eating the soapy eggs.

"You've met Mr. Chapman, dear, haven't you?" said Aunt Sammy as she hoisted herself up onto the counter and stood up in the midst of the smoke.

"She just has to open the vent," said the old man, holding out his left hand as he continued to eat with his right. "Hello, dear. How're the sisters doing without me?" And that was the first time I met the old caretaker man.

"Look, I should get going," I said, as Aunt Sammy smiled down at me though the smoke. I didn't want Joe to know I'd been to that house.

Aunt Sammy climbed down and began to butter the black toast, getting a glob on her glasses. I walked out of the house backward, thanking them both about fifty times.

As I ran from Aunt Sammy's, Mrs. Crain, the guidance counselor, drove up and waved her square hand at me, but I didn't wave back. I decided if I looked anyone in the eye before I got home, I'd turn pregnant or turn into a man. Saint Perpetua was transformed into a man, then fought with the devil and walked on his head.

Not until I was safely sitting on the porch swing could I begin to relax. I figured Mrs. Crain was going to see Aunt Sammy because she wanted to have a baby. Every time Mrs. Flax drove by the Crains' house and saw the baby carriage sitting empty in the garage, she made some comment about how she wished she had such trouble conceiving kids. She was fond of telling us that all she had to do was put her clothes next to a man's clothes in the closet and bingo, she got pregnant, although she did a lot more than that, which we all knew very well.

10

❦

THE WEEK before Christmas, when the snow was level with the top step of our front porch, Mother Superior showed up at the house, trailing her black robes in the white powder and inviting us all to a Christmas party at the convent on Saturday afternoon.

Mrs. Flax told her no, thank you, she had a previous engagement, but said that Kate and I could go if that's the way we really wanted to spend our time. Later she said personally she wouldn't dream of going to an all-woman party, let alone a party consisting mainly of nuns.

Saturday came around like it always did and Kate said if she didn't go swimming she would evaporate.

Mrs. Flax told me, "You can go alone, but I'm going to check in with that head nun later to see that you behaved."

I ironed my navy blue dress three times and decided to wear it backward for a new effect. When I got my ensemble together, I zipped up my vinyl boots and climbed the icy hill to the convent alone. I hesitated at the front gate, kissed the No Trespassing sign, then pinched my cheeks the way Mrs. Flax always did, "to add the blush of youth," as she said, and then I prayed that Joe would be at the party.

The festivities were held in a large stone room off the dining hall, and as I approached through the snow I could hear the nuns laughing in large gales, almost like the sounds of regular grown-ups at a regular party. I walked into the dark corridor and shut my eyes as I put my face in a pile of black cloaks hanging on the wall. I breathed in the incense and strong white soap as I slid my hands into two black pockets. Then I took off my short coat and hung it on top of the nun capes. I smoothed my dress, which seemed to be permanently wrinkled, and then I made my entrance.

The place was jammed with nuns wearing their usual black robes. When my eyes adjusted to the light, I could see several priests threaded through the crowd, each one surrounded by a handful of laughing nuns as if he was a celebrity. There was a long table against the wall, covered with neat rows of Dixie cups full of punch on a green and red reindeer paper tablecloth. I stood by the table, searching for Joe and pretending not to. Finally I saw him, bending over the fireplace, wearing a red flannel shirt, black corduroy pants, and his moccasins. I pinched my cheeks again and walked across the room.

"You need any help, Joe? Mrs. Flax doesn't believe in holidays," I said, stepping so close to the fire I thought my knees would burn. Joe only nodded, and I noticed a small feather sticking out of his shirt pocket. I almost cried, standing there with my stinging knees, and just at the point I thought my boots would melt I wandered off into the crowd. I walked with my palms turned out, touching the nuns' robes, feeling a hand, sometimes a leg, begging for someone to touch me.

Mother Superior's face was flushed with wine, and when she saw me she put her arm around my shoulder, saying to a small circle of nuns, "This young lady is from that nice Jewish family in the house at the bottom of the hill." And all the nuns turned to one another and gave big laughs, like she'd cracked the funniest joke in the Western hemisphere. I pulled away from Mother Superior, put my head down, and ducked into the crowd again. I saw one priest straighten the collar of another priest, and as I reached the door I heard another one say loudly to a knot of nuns that he thought the day would come when there wouldn't be convents, that there would be a time when nuns would wear civilian clothes. He said changes were coming, big changes from Rome.

I walked out into the hallway and yanked down one of the black capes and hung it around my shoulders. It dragged on the floor. I could feel the weight of my sins in the incense, and for several breaths I smelled like a nun. I hung up the cape, then grabbed my coat and ran out of the building into the snow. I heard another explosion of laughter as I tried to run through the drifts to the path that led around the pond, but the snow was deep and I kept falling to my knees.

Finally I got to the path, with snow dripping down in my socks. I followed the path all the way back to the stand of pines. I closed my eyes, slid ten steps, then knelt in the snow in front of the wooden Christ. I had been there before, but I had never told a soul. He hung sadly in the breeze, with nothing on but a ripped piece of cloth carved out of wood.

"Please talk to me," I said.

Then I unzipped my coat and unbuttoned my dress. I

opened it wide, pulled up my bra, and showed him my breasts. "Jesus Christ, look at me, will you?" I whispered, but he didn't make a sound. I quickly covered myself and shouted, "Why do you talk to everyone else?"

Then I picked up a handful of snow in my red hands and packed it as tight as I could into a ball. I put my arm back and hurled it hard at Christ's face, leaving a white splotch of powder over one eye. As soon as I did it, I ran to him and kissed his cold wooden toes.

When I got home Mrs. Flax was in the bathtub. I knocked on the bathroom door and could hear her pull the curtain in front of her.

"Can I come in?"

"If you must."

I walked in and lowered the toilet seat and sat down. I imagined Mrs. Flax was a priest and it was time for me to confess all my sins. I almost screamed out what I'd done in the tower and how I wanted to do more, but instead I took off my vinyl boots and dumped the snow in the sink.

"Well," Mrs. Flax said through the shower curtain. "How is life in the nunnery?" I could hear her splashing around like Kate. "Was our friend Mr. Joe Poseidon there? Was it a swinging party?"

"The nuns were laughing," I said.

"Goodness," said Mrs. Flax, slapping her hand down on the water. "What were they laughing about? What on earth do those women do over there?"

11

THE NEXT DAY I ran away. Mrs. Flax was still getting a ride to work with the nice young man from her office, so I was free to take the car. As soon as Kate got picked up for school I drove off, slinking down behind the steering wheel, acting as small as possible as I drove down Main Street and out onto the highway.

Then I stepped on the gas and drove south with the radio blasting jazz in my ears. "I want to be a whirling dervish! I want a violent and exciting life!" I screamed at the top of my lungs as I almost crashed into a hitchhiker at the side of the road.

At every toll booth I stuck the picture of my father's shoes out the window, but nobody recognized the guy. "Why don't I hear a goddamn voice?" I screamed, honk-honking as I passed every car I could. I couldn't believe I'd ever been attached to Mrs. Flax by my bellybutton. I wanted to have Joe's baby, Joe's second child, and show the whole damn town of Grove. I kept my foot on the gas and my hand on the horn, shouting above Charlie Parker, "Why was I born, O Lord? Why was I put on this earth?"

I ended up in New Jersey, in a blizzard that nearly lost me. It was dark when I took exit something-or-other and slid down streets of a somewhere town, weaving past snow-covered cars that looked like monsters. I can't say I parked. I sort of sidled into a mound of snow, where I sat singing "Onward, Christian Soldiers" to keep warm. I felt like I'd been in that town before, and I pretended I was sitting outside one of our old houses, though there were no wreaths, no plaques, no guides standing guard outside. It was just a little nighttime house in America that looked like it was going to be buried in the snow. I considered freezing to death there. They could have made a shrine out of the car. But I got out and ran to the front door, pounding as hard as I could.

An American father came to the door, wearing slippers and a bathrobe, holding back a golden retriever who was trying to lick off my knees, and I realized I hadn't seen many real-life fathers actually living in their homes. I had seen them in stores or in cars with their kids, but never actually in their bathrobes in the same house as their wives and families. It was not unlike landing on Jupiter.

"Excuse me, sir," I said. "I was out for a spin and I seem to be having some engine trouble."

The American father touched my shoulder and brought me inside.

"I'm a shepherd who's lost my flock," I said.

"Honey!" he called to his wife. "It's all right, it's just a young girl." I stood dripping on the wall-to-wall carpet as he said, "Do your folks know where you are?"

"Sure, my folks know exactly where I am. Especially my dad. He's just that kind of guy."

I ended up sleeping in the den of these nice people's

house, on the couch, next to the Christmas tree, but I didn't get much sleep.

In the morning a gang of kids stood around me on the couch, watching me pretend to sleep. They were giggling and saying shush and stepping on one another's feet. Kate would have liked them, and I considered kidnapping them all.

Breakfast was like a movie. The mother had on an apron and everything and had pretty wavy brown hair. She kept flipping pancakes, and every once in a while she'd stop and look out the window with her spatula up in the air like she was going to have a revelation, but all she said was, "Will you look at that snow come down!" and then she'd go back to the pancakes. They were good pancakes, with a square of butter between each one.

The kids kept asking me where I was from, and I could hear the American father out trying to shovel the driveway. I didn't tell them my boyfriend was twice my age. I mostly told them about my father and how he was probably the son of Rudolph Valentino, and how he'd changed his name to Val, which was my last name. I told them my name was Sal Val. My parents loved rhymes, I said. As a matter of fact, it was our favorite family game, rhyming. We'd stay up late at night, making up rhymes and hugging, all of us together, Dad, Mom, sis, my big brother Al. What could I tell them, we had a great family. I stayed two days with the Americans. They treated me so well I thought they were saving me for some kind of terrible experiment. And the snow kept coming down, as the American mother kept pointing out. It was when I got talking about living in Brazil that the policeman came to take me home. I was just telling the kids about our diamond mine in Brazil, how my grandfather wore diamonds in his eyebrows for decoration. It was no big deal, and my father used to dance with me when I was little. I'd stand on a big box that was inlaid with diamonds, way out in the middle of the jungle, and we'd dance and dance. And I told them about my little sister, who wore a little diamond crown on her red curls, and how we used to make pear wine and hang the bottles on the tree branches and write on the bottles with diamond dust. Actually, that was the exact point the policeman showed up, and another cop, with a pie face and braces on his teeth, drove behind in the station wagon all the way back to Grove.

When I finally got home late that night, Mrs. Flax didn't say a word. She just stood in the kitchen with one hand on her waist and pointed to the atlas, which was open on the kitchen table to the Hindu Kush. Kate seemed pretty glad to see me and said I could borrow her *Fish of the World* encyclopedia whenever I wanted.

The next morning I overheard Mrs. Flax on the phone with Lou, saying, "I don't know, maybe I should send the girl to that counselor at school, Mrs. Crain, as much of a horse's ass as the woman is." But nothing ever panned out with that.

Kate and I crept around the house like gangsters that day, waiting for Mrs. Flax to come home and tell us to pack our bags, but she got distracted by the New Year's invitation in the mail.

It seemed that every year Mr. and Mrs. Crain had a New Year's Eve party, a costume party, and every year they sent out the same invitation with a reindeer playing a tuba and the words of the invitation coming out of the horn like musical notes. When Mrs. Flax received her invitation she immediately threw it away, saying celebrating New Year's was like counting steps to your grave, but on December 31st we realized she'd changed her mind. We heard her rummaging around in her closet, so we went and sat on her bed to see if she was throwing everything away again.

"Maybe she's going to throw us away," whispered Kate, as Mrs. Flax pulled a large sequined costume out of the closet.

"Mermaid," she said, holding it up as if it were a normal dress.

The amazing part of the costume was you could step into it and zip it all the way from the bottom, or leave it slightly open, with its rubber fin in back, so you could walk. It was a fairly complicated outfit, with an intricate series of zippers. Mrs. Flax told us that she had called in sick to work one day and taken a train all the way to a costume store in the city. After trying on gorilla and vampire heads in the hot dressing room, she emerged from behind the curtain as a mermaid. The man who ran the store, who said he wore a different costume every day, was dressed as a crocodile. Each time Mrs. Flax appeared in a different outfit he told her she looked like a million dollars, so she had to decide on the mermaid costume on her own.

We sat on the bed, watching her try to squeeze the costume on over her slip. She wasn't fat, that wasn't the problem. She had plenty of curves but she wasn't fat. It was just too much with the slip, so she made us turn around while she pulled the slip up over her head.

Then she bent down and crawled into the closet. This time she came out with a curly green wig as calmly as if she were the sort of woman who always had odd costumes and wigs lying around. In fact, she'd told us many times that she thought costumes were some of the most embarrassing inventions of the human race. On Halloween we never dressed in funny clothes. She never even bought candy for other children who showed up, and one year she gave out small tubes of toothpaste.

"I don't think you need the hair," said Kate the moment Mrs. Flax put on the wig.

"Of course I need the hair," she said, turning from side to side with her hand on her hip. "I'm a mermaid."

"Are you going to drive in that?" I asked.

"See? I can zip it like this," she said, zipping the costume tightly around her ankles and falling onto the bed, "or I can keep it open. I think I'll be a hit."

"You're going to get arrested," I said.

"And what are your plans for the evening?" said Mrs. Flax. "I heard one of the girls in your class, Pam or Shirley or someone, is giving a party. Did you get invited?"

"Yes, I got invited," I said. I'd never gotten invited to a party in Grove. "I just don't think I'm in the mood."

"You really should go," said Mrs. Flax, pulling all her purses out of the closet and dumping them on the bed. "Which one should I bring?"

"Don't bring a purse," said Kate. "Mermaids don't carry purses."

"This is fine," said Mrs. Flax, holding up a patent leather bag. "Do I look all right?"

Mrs. Flax stood in her mermaid costume in front of the mirror, putting on a new pink lipstick that Carrie had talked her into.

"Is that thing waterproof?" said Kate, touching Mrs. Flax's sequined stomach.

"I rather doubt it, sweetheart, so don't get any ideas,"

said Mrs. Flax, rubbing her lips together. "It really is a wonderful costume, don't you think? Maybe if I'd had this when you two were little I'd have worn it, you know, washing diapers or ironing. Look, I'll show you."

Mrs. Flax took tiny steps into the bathroom and we followed after her. She tried to kneel at the tub but ended in more of a hunch. She picked up the sponge and circled her hand in the air, pretending to clean the tub.

"See, it adds a little life to the most dreary of household tasks."

I looked at Kate behind her back and mouthed the word "nutso," and Kate burst out laughing.

"What's so funny?" said Mrs. Flax.

"Nothing," I said, biting down on a smile.

"You are," giggled Kate, pointing to the wig.

"What?" Mrs. Flax stood up and looked at herself in the mirror. "God in heaven," she said, laughing as she stepped into the tub. She slid down until she was sitting, laughing and shaking her green curls. Then I began to laugh for the first time in about a century. Kate was having a complete giggling fit and climbed right into the tub and sat down on Mrs. Flax's lap. I took off my boots and got in, kneeling in front of Kate. The three of us were packed into the tub, almost in tears, and Kate only had to say "A purse? A mermaid with a purse?" to make us all crack up again.

"We're on a mermaid bus," I shouted, holding on to the faucet, and then we all laughed some more.

The phone rang but we barely heard it through our giggles. Mrs. Flax finally dried her eyes and said, "I guess it's time to answer the mermaid phone," and she stood up as gracefully as she could.

We followed her into the kitchen, laughing quietly now.

It was a quick conversation. Mrs. Flax wasn't laughing at all when she got off the line. She held on to the edge of the sink with her sequined hands. "That was your father," she said, looking at me. "He's going to pay us a little visit in the spring. Let's not discuss it anymore," and then Kate and I stopped laughing too.

We followed her back into the bedroom. For some reason we all knew that this time he really was going to show up.

"Do you think I need a coat with this outfit?" said Mrs. Flax as she held up a string of pearls to her sequined throat.

"You'd look dumb with a coat," Kate said solemnly.

"I should get going." Mrs. Flax picked up her coat and black patent leather purse and stepped into her high heels. We followed her out onto the porch and waved to her as she plodded through the snow to the car. She honked when she drove off with her fin tail sticking out under the door.

Kate and I went back inside and stared at a plate of Chicken Liver and Water Chestnut Delites she had left on the kitchen table.

"Do you think he's really coming?" said Kate.

"This time's no dress rehearsal," I said. "There was just something about how quiet she got on the phone. C'mon, we need some air," and I pulled her back out to the porch.

It was a clear, icy night and the moon was glaring white in the sky. Kate began jumping up and down.

"Here, you stop jumping and we can sit on the swing," I said, brushing off the snow with my sleeve. "C'mon."

We sat on the cold, damp porch swing and swung back and forth.

"The last day, ever, ever, ever of this year," said Kate.

"You want to make some resolutions, you know, wishes?"

"My revolution is to swim forever," said Kate. "And go inside so I don't turn into a Frigidaire."

"O.K., sorry. I wish I'd known Anne Frank."

And I wished I was pure enough to take the veil and I wished I didn't covet Joe so much.

"Good-bye, year," said Kate, waving out into the night. "I'm staying up 'til she gets home."

Ten minutes later she fell asleep on my shoulder, and I picked her up and carried her inside. I stretched her out on the couch and covered her with a blanket, then went back out and sat on the swing. The convent bell didn't ring that night, and I worried that Joe was sick. Fireworks sputtered red and yellow in the distance. "Happy New Year, Happy New Year, American family," I whispered. I swung faster and put my hands in fists inside my pockets.

I must have fallen asleep because the next thing I knew a car drove in, crunching the snow. I sat up and covered my eyes from the glaring headlights. The icy trees clattered like ladders in the wind.

"Mom?" I called.

The headlights went off but the motor was still running. I squinted in the dark but couldn't see who it was. "Mom?"

The passenger door opened and Mrs. Flax's laugh echoed across the yard as she stepped a high-heeled foot into the snow.

"Charlotte, is that you up so late? Mr. Peretti was a gentleman and drove me home. Wouldn't you know, car's stuck back at the Crains'."

Mrs. Flax tripped up the steps, carrying her wig in one hand, the black patent leather purse in the other. The headlights went on again and I covered my eyes.

"Aren't you going to say hello?" she asked. "He's such

a sweet man. I'll tell you a secret. I kissed him on the cheek."

"Are you kidding?" I said as Joe drove off.

"Shush, Charlotte. It's New Year's, why not? Where's your sister?"

"She's asleep. I thought you didn't believe in New Year's," I screamed.

"Shush, you'll wake your sister," shouted Mrs. Flax, filling the cold air with her wine breath.

"You kissed him? I don't believe you did that!"

"Will you keep it down. Do you want to wake the nuns?" said Mrs. Flax.

"What did he do?"

"Oh he's shy, very shy, one of the shyest men I've ever met."

"You shouldn't have done that," I said.

"Oh, for God's sake, it was just a New Year's kiss."

The hall light went on and Kate stepped into the doorway. The white light surrounded her as if she were an angel, and she stood rubbing her eyes.

"What are you fighting about, you guys?"

"Nothing," said Mrs. Flax.

"Everything," I said.

"Can I get a word in eggwise?" said Kate.

"I was a dancing mermaid," said Mrs. Flax. "Now get into the house before you freeze," and she gently pushed Kate inside.

"Do you intend to stay out here forever, Charlotte?" she muttered.

I ran down the steps and picked up a handful of snow and threw it out into the dark. I did it again, bending down, scooping handfuls, packing them, and then throwing the snowballs, until my fingers were freezing, then burning, and then I couldn't feel them at all. I picked up more snow, not bothering to pack it, just throwing the snow loose so it flew back at me, and I stumbled up the porch steps into the house.

1964

12

THE FIRST DAY of the new year I stayed in my room until Mrs. Flax left the house, and at two in the afternoon I walked up the hill to confess my evil ways to Mother Superior.

I stood at the entrance to the convent, as the wind rattled the bars of the gate. The place looked more deserted than usual; Joe had told me that fewer and fewer women were joining the order and more and more were leaving each year, but I never saw one of them go. I thought the nuns must be stealing away in the darkest shadows of the night, because I never saw them hurrying along the paths with their skirts lifted above their ankles. I never saw one dash into a waiting sedan with its motor running at the gate. What I finally decided was that some of the nuns must have fled while they were outside the convent. Maybe one day after teaching at the Catholic school in the next town, a nun had erased the blackboard for the last time after dismissing her class, then she'd snuck into the girls' locker room with a small bag of clothes she'd bought secretly at the store. She'd told the salesgirl that the dress and slip were presents for her niece. "Yes, my niece is exactly my size." And then the nun had stuffed her habit into a gym locker and walked away in normal clothes and nun shoes, never to be heard of at the convent again. Or maybe a nun had taken the train all the way into the city and checked into an ugly old hotel, where she'd changed into her regular clothes, checked out, and dumped her habit at the nearest cleaners, telling the man who ran the place that the pope was coming to town and she needed her habit extra-specially clean. Then the nun had thrown away the receipt. But whatever I imagined, I never actually saw one of the sisters leaving the convent for the final time. I wondered if some day an ex-nun's messy kids would bump into the black robes stuffed in the back of the closet.

I shook the bars of the gate. I was going to fight for God and my people. I talked to my troops, sitting tall in the saddle, reminding them to hold their swords close to their sides as they rode, and then I entered the convent. I took giant strides in the deep snow, down the path toward Mother Superior's cottage. I'd never been there before. I'd only seen it from the tower. But once when she'd driven by while I was standing in the middle of our yard, staring straight up at the sun, she'd stopped the car and walked over to me, put her hand on my shoulder, and said in a quiet voice, "Charlotte, if there's ever anything you would like to discuss, please feel free to knock on my door."

I wanted to confess that I was berserk in love, and I wanted to tell her how strong his arms felt around me. I wanted to confess that I'd been waiting for my father to come back since the day I was born, and what did she think about that. If she really wanted to know, I was going to tell her I didn't believe for a minute I was ever just a crazy piece of sperm and egg growing inside Mrs. Flax. I was going to ask her very simply, in a calm voice, if she happened to have any hints — not tricks, but suggestions — on how to have a holy soul. I would swear I wouldn't spread what she said around. If she had the time I was going to tell her about the new book on Simone Weil I was reading, and how I didn't like to say it out loud but I was beginning to wonder if Simone had been permanently out to lunch, and I was beginning to think the trillion earthly TV antennas had jammed the airwaves so I'd never hear a voice from on high.

I stood on the doorstep to her cottage and knocked twice, crossing myself in between. The cottage was identical to Joe's on the outside, stone with ivy crawling up the side. There was a metal mailbox next to the door, with its tongue hanging open full of snow. There was a small red cross on it, instead of a little flag, to put up if you wanted to send out a letter, and I wondered if we could put one of those on the mailbox at home. I could hear a chair scrape across the floor, and a moment later Mother Superior was filling the doorway, the wind blowing crumbs down her large chest.

"Why, Charlotte! Hello, dear, is everything all right? You must be freezing. Please come inside."

I stepped in and stood dripping by the door.

"Don't worry about those," she said, looking at my boots. "If you would be more comfortable, please take them off."

I wasn't more comfortable in or out of my boots. I felt like weeping, but I decided to take them off. I leaned against the door, trying to do the whole thing as neatly as possible. There was a fire burning in the fireplace, and I felt dizzy it was so hot. As I bent over to pull off my boots, I glanced around the place. Books evenly lined the shelves; if I squinted so I couldn't see the orange textbooks used by the nuns at Catholic school, the whole place had the feel of a regular house. There was a kitchen table, not wood like the one Joe had, but white metal, which looked like it had been there since the Civil War. The blue sugar bowl was placed exactly in the center, and there were crumbs scattered across the surface. There were no pictures on the walls, which were painted plain white, but there was a small crucifix above the stove. In the corner was a black umbrella.

"Please sit down," said Mother Superior, as if she was a regular woman, and I sat at one of the two metal chairs.

"Would you like some hot chocolate? You must be cold."

As she moved around from the refrigerator to the stove, I tried to see if her movements were different from any other woman, if she gave off some holy light, but I couldn't really tell. She did seem fatter than she did outside, as if she was filling a miniature house, demonstrating how to make hot chocolate on a toy stove. Mother Superior opened the cupboard and took out a royal blue tin of rich Danish butter cookies, then poured us each a cup of hot chocolate and set the food down on the table. I had a strong feeling that she had put the cookie tin back in the cupboard only a few minutes before. There was something so familiar about the way her fingers opened the tin, and of course there were those crumbs all over the table.

I began to tell Mother Superior, though in not so many words, how I wasn't exactly certain what I planned to do when I graduated from school. Under my breath I said something about wanting peace and passion, as she rustled through the white papers in the cookie tin and nodded. When she didn't give me any advice, I took one sip of the hot chocolate and burned the roof of my mouth. The cottage was so warm I wondered if she ever took off her habit and sat around in her underwear. I got so nervous that I began to eat the cookies, too. Between us we rustled through both layers of white paper in the tin in a very short time.

At school, lists had been passed out, lists of professions and jobs in the real world. I knew what was available, but I just didn't feel I was destined to be anything they mentioned, not archaeologist or zoologist, and saint was not on the list at all. I was going to ask Mother Superior how long it would take to be a nun if you weren't Catholic, but she stood up and brushed the crumbs from the table into her hand like a waitress and threw them into the fire. I didn't know if I was supposed to start genuflecting or help clean up, so I sat staring into the orange flames. I was about to thank her and leave and run to the tower and find Joe, but then she took down another tin of cookies and set it on the table. We started again on the top layer, and I tried to chew as silently as a martyr.

I sat listening to the ice creaking in the frozen pond, and Mother Superior began to make little designs in the crumbs with her fingers. At first I didn't see what she was doing, but then I realized she was making rows of crumb crosses in lines across the table. I decided I would count them, and if Mother Superior still hadn't said a word when I was finished, still hadn't given me the secret to a holy life, then I would thank her very much for her hospitality and leave. I hit twenty-three, and suddenly Mother Superior began to talk. Her head was bent down so that at first I wasn't sure if she was praying or doing some special sort of meditation. I leaned in to catch her words, then looked away, out the window to the pond. I was suddenly embarrassed, as if Mother Superior was confessing to me, but it didn't seem to matter where I looked; she was on automatic pilot.

She began in a low voice, about her family, how she had entered the convent when she was only sixteen years old and how different everything had been in those days, how terribly strict. She described the white dress she wore when she took her vows, and she even put her hands lightly on her shoulders to demonstrate the style, like she was describing her wedding dress. They all wore white dresses back then, she said, when they were married to Christ. She said she was so excited she couldn't eat that day, but when she had first told her brother, whom she still missed every single minute of the day, that she had decided to become a nun, he had tried to talk her out of it. No matter how much she prayed and prayed, she told me, she didn't miss her brother any less, and it was very possible that in recent years, she said, she had begun to miss him more.

I didn't know whether she wanted me to ask what happened to her brother at that point, so I grabbed a butter cookie and licked it, but she kept talking. She went on to tell me about all the changes there'd been over the years in Grove, how for years all the stores had stood in their peeling paint and splintered wood, with many of the houses completely boarded up. She told of what it was like long before, when she entered the convent, how the town had bustled, and then of the empty years when most of the stores were closed. She grew up in a town fifty miles north of Grove, but she considered Grove her real home. She said she remembered when the Peretti family moved into our house down the hill, how she had first met Joe's father when he was out painting their name on the mailbox, and for a moment I thought she was going to say she knew what a sinner I'd been with Joe. But she didn't; instead, she blushed slightly and said that now there was this "renaissance" Mr. Landsky kept talking about. She talked as if she was in a trance, jumping around from subject to subject, and I thought we were getting closer to something from above.

The snow blew against the window panes, and finally I breathed out, as quietly as I could. As she talked, she pushed the crumbs into more crosses with her puffy fingers, until the whole kitchen table looked like a miniature cemetery. She said she had trouble believing it, but with the chaos going on around the world, and what was being said at meetings she attended in the city, soon there might not be any convents at all.

"I remember my first day here," she said. "My mother and father brought me and there was a picnic by the pond. Everyone was so frightened and hung together with their families. My brother didn't come, though. He thought I was foolish. You would have liked my brother. He was a wonderful boy. Sometimes Joseph reminds me of him."

I didn't know where to look, but Mother Superior kept her head bent most of the time so it didn't matter. I could have even knocked the whole tin of cookies to the floor, and still she wouldn't have looked up. Suddenly I felt like telling her everything about my life, what I had seen, about my past. I wanted to tell her about driving with Mrs. Flax through Texas, how we'd seen a wind-ripped poster on the side of a barn that said EAT LAMB, when we'd gone to visit one of her gentleman friends at the end of a wide dirt road. I wanted to tell Mother Superior everything I'd ever seen or heard, and instead I tried to put my face into a small smile and listened to her confess.

I grabbed another cookie when Mother Superior said that everything was taken away when they entered the convent, their names, their hair, so they didn't own one single thing. Everything was given up to Christ, everything, and she said they were supposed to spend their whole lives repenting for all their sins.

I closed one eye and listened to Mother Superior talk about the importance of being "called" and the grace of vocation. I wanted to scream that I had tried for years to hear the Word, but I kept quiet and listened as she explained that everything was done for Him, from washing in the icy water in bowls near their beds every morning to carrying around little black books to write down their faults so they would remember to meditate on each sin.

Mother Superior suddenly lifted her head and held up her thumbs. "They even made us put a little piece of paper under our thumbnails so when we turned the pages of our prayer books we wouldn't soil the pages, but that stopped years ago. My brother thought it was all very foolish." And finally she began to talk about her brother. He was killed between the wars. Nobody knew exactly what happened, but he had joined the army as a career man when he was seventeen years old; they sent him home a year later in pieces in a box.

"You would have liked my brother," she said again. "The joints of the day, dawn and dusk, those are the loneliest, don't you think?" and I opened both eyes and nodded.

She said she remembered her brother best in the cold

New England winters. He would pretend to smoke a cigarette by puffing his breath through two fingers. That was the picture she always carried of him in her head. Their favorite game as children, which was her brother's idea, was to find new smells in the world and add them to a list they never wrote down. Mother Superior smiled as she remembered going to the grocery store with her brother and racing around the aisles, trying to smell every kind of food there was. Whoever could stand closest to the grocer's garlicky hands was the winner of the day. They had a gardener come to their home once a year to prune the trees and shrubs, and he always brought extra sandwiches, greasy salami sandwiches. Mother Superior and her brother, when they were children, sat as close to his hands as they could on the front lawn, eating the hard-roll sandwiches as crumbs fell into the flowers.

Before her brother enlisted in the army, he had one job that he liked. He found work in a store, a wholesale place in the city, where cooks and restaurant people went to choose spices from wooden barrels. Her brother always came home with paprika on his shoes, and he used to bring her cinnamon sticks and put them underneath her pillow. The smells made her brother dizzy, but instead of adjusting as the boss told him he would, he found he could barely concentrate as he scooped the spices from the barrels. One morning when a cook from an Indian restaurant arrived in his chef's hat and sandals, her brother spilled a gold brick's worth of saffron all over the tiled floor. It was then that he was fired, and soon after he joined the army. Mother Superior was in the convent by then.

Mother Superior suddenly pushed back her chair and stood up. "Here, I'll show you something," she said.

I thought that she was going to show me some photographs of her brother in uniform, or when he was a little boy and crazy about smells. I stood up and left half a cookie on my chair and followed Mother Superior into her bedroom. The room was as simple and neat as you would expect, with one narrow bed with a black blanket beneath a cross on the wall. A tall bureau stood in the corner like a soldier. There was a floor-to-ceiling bookcase full of all kinds of books, not just religious ones, but poetry and novels that I didn't think a nun was allowed to read.

Mother Superior bent down on her knees by the bed and I thought she was going to ask me to join her in silent prayer or tell me about the sin of being a Jew, but instead she said, "I haven't done this in many years." She reached under the bed and pulled out a dusty suitcase with gold initials stamped near the handle. She dragged it into the center of the floor and knelt in front of it as if she had just discovered buried treasure. I thought, This is it, she is going to perform some sort of repulsive sacrifice.

"This is what I brought into the convent with me, goodness, how many years ago? I'm sixty. I was sixteen. How's your math, Charlotte?"

To be honest my mathematical abilities were probably the same as Cro-Magnon man's, so I let her calculate. "Forty-four years," she said, and I nodded. "That's right, forty-four."

Mother Superior looked frightened, as if she might be punished for what she was about to do, and she hesitated in front of the suitcase. I stood over her and suddenly wanted to stroke the top of her head, to feel the black material, but I kept my hands tightly at my sides.

The fire cracked in the next room while Mother Superior

slowly pulled herself up onto one leg and then the other, as if she had changed her mind. She stood up and I thought she might be going back for more cookies, but she went over to the bureau and slowly pulled open the top drawer. She lifted out a black satin ribbon threaded through a small key, and I wondered if she ever roller-skated as a child. For a moment, when the drawer was open, I thought I could smell cinnamon, but she shut it quickly so there was no way to tell. She wrapped the ribbon around her fingers and said there actually had been a discussion about what color the ribbon should be, although her mother had said right away that of course it had to be black. Mother Superior told me how nervous she had been that day, waiting for her own mother to thread the black ribbon through the little hole in the key. Finally her brother trimmed it with a scissors to make it fit. I wanted to ask why she had the suitcase at all if she was supposed to have given up all her worldly goods, but I kept quiet.

She knelt down again in front of the suitcase, with the key in the palm of her hand. She said her mother had put the ribbon around her neck the last day she lived at home, and then kissed her on the forehead. Her father only touched her lightly on the back. Earlier, her brother had yelled at her, which was something he never did, saying she was making the worst mistake of her life. But on the actual day of her leaving he didn't say one word. He just lifted the suitcase off her bed and quietly carried it downstairs to the front door.

Mother Superior didn't open the suitcase immediately. She stayed on her knees, with me staring down at her, and she told me how difficult it was at first, not only for the first few days, but for years after taking the vows of poverty, chastity, and obedience, even though she knew it was her vocation to be with God and to live in the convent. I chewed on my lips and wanted to ask her if God had ever really spoken to her, and I wanted to tell her what I had done with Joe.

Finally she put the key in the lock of the suitcase, and as she did, she burst out, saying it was almost unbearable to live without her brother. I was frightened to see her so upset and tried to change the subject by saying, "I hope the key fits," in a cheerful voice. The key turned and Mother Superior lifted the leather top. There weren't jewels and coins inside, only clothes, just the way she had packed them away when she'd taken her vows years before. The navy blue pleated skirt was lying flat across the top, and there were the white blouse and white gloves, which had turned an uneven beige. She lifted up each piece and carefully laid them on the bed, as if she was going out on a date that night. There were even old-fashioned shoes with rows of difficult buttons.

The clothes looked like they might fit me. They were definitely too small for her, and I realized she hadn't always been at those tins of cookies. She seemed like a ship in a bottle somehow, too big to possibly ever get out the way she had gotten in. I stood looking down at the clothes and suddenly felt very tired. I wanted to lie down on the bed and hibernate for the rest of the winter, but I stood as straight as I could, picturing Mother Superior as a young girl, scared to give up her life, scared of God, so homesick, standing by the pond in those old-fashioned clothes.

She shook her head, then carefully began to fold everything exactly the way she had folded it when she was a teenager and put everything neatly back in the suitcase, exactly the way it was. She locked the suitcase and brushed crumbs down her habit, then dropped the key back in the bureau drawer. I looked out the window and realized it was just another cold January first, of a whole, entire other year.

I followed Mother Superior back into the kitchen and decided it was definitely time to leave. It would be getting dark soon, and I felt I had heard too much already.

"More hot chocolate?" said Mother Superior, holding up the kettle.

I didn't refuse, and before I knew it there we were like magnets at the kitchen table again, starting on another round of cookies. I decided I would tell Mother Superior about living all over the country in eighteen different houses, but before I could open my mouth she began talking again about some man. At first I thought it was more stories about her brother, how wonderful he was, but she wasn't using her brother's name at all. She wasn't talking about some priest; no. She was talking about Mr. Landsky. She wasn't making much sense, and at first I thought she had just said his name by mistake, but it really was Lou Landsky, Mrs. Flax's beau of shoe-store fame, she was getting so excited about. She was talking about when she first met him, when she was in her thirties. I had trouble picturing it, but as a substitute teacher in Oklahoma once told our class, "If you can imagine it, then it's happened somewhere, no matter how bee-zarre it seems." What Mother Superior was saying, without a smile on her face, was that she had been in love with Mr. Landsky, once. She skipped around the subject a lot, talking more about her brother and how he should never have enlisted, but then she got back to Mr. Landsky. She said she had written him hundreds of letters over the years but had never mailed them. Instead, each time she wrote a letter, which was many times more often than once a week, she would build a fire and burn it in the fireplace, even on muggy days in summer, and I thought of Lou holding Mother Superior's foot in his hand.

Mother Superior was not looking for my blessing, though, and continued to talk about what a handsome man he was. "I loved the way he straightened his glasses," she said. I stared into the fire, wondering if there were bits of love sentences in the corners of the fireplace, charred "darling"s and blackened "I love you forever"s, but all I saw were the crumpled white papers from all the cookies.

Finally she stopped talking and I said, "Thank you for listening to me, Reverend Mother."

"Please come back any time, you're always welcome to come and talk if you have anything on your mind," she said, as if she had snapped out of a trance.

I nodded and slid back my chair.

"Would you like some cookies to bring home to your mother and sister?"

'No, no thank you, they're on diets." I stepped into my boots and put on my damp coat.

"No hat or gloves?"

"No, Reverend Mother. I don't need them, thank you very much."

I walked out into the wind toward the pond, the cold air freezing in my nose. I tacked back and forth through the snow and headed toward the tower.

If Mother Superior and Mrs. Flax could be in love with Lou Landsky, I was going to declare my love to Joe. I was sick of lying. I was sick of thinking everything I did was a sin. If Mother Superior sinned, why couldn't I? I climbed the stone steps two at a time and found Joe sitting up there, bundled up on the bench.

I stood right in front of him, blocking his view.

"Did my mother kiss you?" I said.

"Charlotte, you've got to stop. I can't stand it. I hate New Year's anyway."

"Well, I hate you, Joe. I really do."

Joe stood up and I thought he was going to throw me over the wall, but he moved toward the bell and grabbed the icy rope, pulling it as hard as he could, so the bell began to clang, echoing in the wind.

"You're going to get in trouble," I said.

"Trouble? Who from? God?" shouted Joe into the cold air.

"Did you wear a costume last night?" I said.

He continued to ring the bell furiously. "This place is falling apart," he said. "Nobody wants to be a nun anymore. Nobody wants to wear black and be good." He rang harder and harder until it looked like the bell would drop into the snow.

"She kisses everyone, did you know that? You're not so great!" I shouted. "Why did you let her? What about us?"

Joe kept ringing. I waited for the nuns to appear, fluttering out of the dormitory, their black robes swirling in the snow to see what was going on. I waited for them to see what was going on with the lunatic caretaker man.

"Did I ever tell you about the town my father took me to when I was a kid, way out in the country?" said Joe, still ringing the bell.

"She doesn't really like you. She doesn't really like anybody. You're nobody special!"

"I don't remember why we were there," said Joe as he clanged the bell. "Houses were renting for one dollar a year 'cause they were rerouting a river over the place. The whole town was going to be washed away."

I covered my ears and hummed "Silent Night." I was thinking about the New Year's Eve party at the Crains'. I could just see them all with their shoes off, dancing around. The pillows were probably off the big couches, scattered all over the floor. Lou probably made everyone do the cha-cha, and maybe Joe grabbed Mrs. Flax's mermaid waist and wiggled with her through the crowd.

13

THE SHOE STORE saved me that winter. I spent hours in the back with Lou, standing by the radiator, as he told stories about keeping kosher in South Dakota. I breathed in the licorice and shoe-leather smell and could almost forget the snow that covered the town and the fact I'd felt cold all my life. I told Lou what I knew about my father and even described his shoes, but he said he hadn't seen them around. When Lou went to the front of the store to help customers, I'd quickly lift each shoe to my ear, the old caretaker's old work boots, Aunt Sammy's funny red flats — I held all the shoes to my ear but all I could hear was the hiss of the radiator.

One Saturday morning in March I woke up to hear Mrs. Flax jabbering on the phone. For a second I thought, This is it, Our Father Who Art in Heaven has returned. He's at the train station. I'll go pick him up and show him the town and we'll all live happily ever after. I got out of bed and hid, watching Mrs. Flax from behind the kitchen door. She was sitting on the table, wrapping the telephone cord around her as if it was a mink stole.

"Why, that sounds like it's just what I need," she said. I wanted to pick up one of the chairs and throw it at her head.

"No," she said. "They'll be all right here alone."

I felt free. The woman was finally abandoning us for good. My wings had been taped back and suddenly I was going to fly. I wanted to run into the kitchen and yank the phone from her hand, but she kept chattering in a way that made me realize it wasn't Mr. Flax at all.

"Oh, no, I'd love to watch those boys train in the bull-pen, Lou. Nothing would make me happier."

When she finally hung up she stayed sitting on the table, swinging her legs back and forth.

I stayed behind the door and said as calmly as I could, "What the hell was that all about?"

She began to talk about how she loved baseball, saying it really was her one true passion. She didn't know a line drive from a catcher's mitt, but she talked on, saying she was going on the most wonderful trip in the world. Lou had invited her to drive all the way down to Florida with him to watch the rookies play at spring training.

"In the bullpen, can you imagine," she said. "You two will be all right without me for a while."

She hadn't been seeing Lou for several weeks, and I'd begun to think he'd been mysteriously discarded with the rest of the men, but then there he was on the telephone, for some reason wanting to spend a thousand hours in a car with her. For years he'd been talking to everyone in town about someday going down to spring training. Apparently the idea started when he was very young. He'd stand in the middle of the driveway, pounding his baseball mitt, talking

about a caravan of cars heading south. He said the other
boys always nodded but nobody took him seriously.

When Lou arrived to pick up Mrs. Flax the next morning, she appeared in a cotton dress under her winter coat,
even though there was a raw wind blowing hard against the
porch.

"Yoo-hoo," she yelled, running down the steps into the
snow. "Take me out to the ball game."

That night I made two cakes as a treat for Kate. After
we were already stuffed from licking the frosting bowls,
vanilla and butterscotch, we took the cakes out onto the
porch and sat on the swing with our coats on, each with a
cake on our lap.

"What would you do if I moved away?" I said.

"Did Dad leave because I was born?" said Kate.

"Of course not, he adores you. Here, let's switch plates.
You'll see what a great guy he is when he gets here."

"You're so full of baloney," said Kate.

We stayed up late that night until we were both so sick
of cake we swore we would never eat again. Then Kate
gave a short speech on the importance of schools of fish
and I told her the story of Christ's birth for the millionth
time.

"I don't think he liked those presents they brought him
when he was a baby," said Kate. "Frankenstein and birds.
I think he wanted a dump truck."

I suddenly thought that my father would like Kate much
better than me when he showed up. I was scared I wouldn't
have to take him aside and whisper in his ear that he should
be especially nice to Kate and pretend he was her real
father. I was scared he would fall madly in love with Kate
and disown me the second he walked onto the porch.

Kate took one last bite of butterscotch cake and sucked

on her fork. After five minutes of sitting like that she said, "I think I'm going to retire for the evening," and got up and went inside.

I sat out on the swing, swinging in the wet breeze, and soon it began to rain, the very first rain of the year. They weren't snowflakes coming down but drip-dripping raindrops, a cold rain, pelting the roof of the house and the car and the steps. Soon people would be saying they would prefer the snow back — at least the snow was clean, at least it looked pretty — but there was no going back. The March rains had come. It would rain day and night, night and day, raining cats and dogs to beat the band. I put down the last wedges of cake and contemplated throwing them out into the front yard. At eleven-thirty the rain was coming down so hard I was worried all the roads would flood, even the roads down to Florida. I was worried Mrs. Flax would come home early. I watched the rain slide down the dark pines and I thought I was finally being treated to an epiphany, when Joe Peretti appeared on the bottom step, wearing his black slicker and rubber boots, looking like a fisherman.

"Ma'am," he whispered. "I hear your mother's away."

He shook himself off and sat down next to me on the squeaking swing. The lights were all out in the house, but I wasn't sure if Kate was asleep or pretending to be, or whether she was taking a bath in the dark, which she'd begun to do recently.

Joe shut his eyes. It was maple syrup time and he was exhausted to his bones.

And then he said he wanted to tell me something. I thought he was going to tell me that he knew that Mother Superior loved Lou, but he said he wanted to tell me about his high school girlfriend. He said she was a cheerleader, which I'd already heard, and I said I wasn't impressed. He asked if I'd kindly let him talk, and then he said she moved away in the middle of senior year, which I also knew. I thought he was going to finally tell the truth about whether there was a Joey, Jr., walking around, but he started telling me about driving her out to the hills in his father's car one rainy night. Just hearing him mention another girl made my stomach hurt but I sat on my hands and let him talk. He said that for a few seconds he switched off the lights and drove in the dark. It was like swimming in a lake at night. His girlfriend had shrieked, "Joseph, stop," and grabbed his hand. Later, when Joe parked the car at an overlook, she said she would get undressed if he did first, and I said I really had no interest in hearing this particular part of the story. Joe got angrier than I'd ever seen him and said, "Damn it, would you let me talk! I've been wanting to tell someone this for years." So he said he had slowly pulled off his clothes, throwing them in the back seat, until he sat naked, clutching the steering wheel, staring out through the fogged windshield. But then she turned on the inside light and giggled.

"Yes?" I said.

"'Yes?' What do you mean 'yes?'" said Joe. I thought he was going to strangle me.

"But what about the baby?" I said.

"No baby, no nothing. She moved a week later. Nothing happened. It never did. Don't you understand anything?"

Ever since, he said, he wore too many clothes, layers of shirts and thick socks, always feeling too hot, sweating in every season. And the town kept talking, he said, talking and talking, making him into some kind of Don Juan, and nothing had happened. After his friends went off to college or the army, he said, he spent his evenings at old movies in the next town, in a theater where men came from all the neighboring towns and sat hunched, with wet eyes, watching movie stars fall in love. Once, he said, once he went to the woman who kept a room upstairs from the Dream Castle Bar, next door to the theater, but it hadn't worked out well.

Then he said, "The Algonquins, they had rites of passage." I put my hand on his knee, but he lifted it by the wrist and gently put it back in my own lap.

"I think I should move to Florida," he said.

"Terrific. Why doesn't everyone move to Florida? That way you'll be closer to Mrs. Flax in the damn bullpen."

"No, I really should get out of this town. I used to be alive. I used to be able to play football." And then he told me how he helped his father tap the maple trees behind the house when he was a boy. Every year they ruined their clothes with the sticky sap, and every year his father made the same joke about the trees being like women. Every year his father would also help the old caretaker with tapping the trees in the convent, and he said Mother Superior always came out to watch. Joe had done all the work alone this year, lugging the full buckets, building the fire, stirring the thick sap down into syrup.

"You want to spend the night, Joe?" I said.

"D'you have any oil for this swing?" he said.

I hurried into the kitchen and got the can of 3-in-1 Oil from under the sink. I considered locking the door and leaving him on the porch, but I missed him and quickly went back outside.

As Joe oiled the squeaking joints of the swing, he said, "I remember when my father drove my sisters and me one night when it was raining like this. The roads were like lacquer. I sat in the back seat, crushed between the girls, and my father looked through the rainy windshield past the rabbit's foot hanging from the mirror. 'Joey,' my father said, 'Joey, how much is five times seven?' and my sisters screamed the answer before I even had a chance to open my mouth."

Joe sat back down next to me on the swing. The squeak was gone.

He took off his rain slicker. This is it, I thought. He's going to take me in his arms and rip off my buttons. But within a few minutes he'd fallen asleep with his head on my shoulder. I continued to swing, pretending he was my child. An hour passed, rocking, rocking on the swing. Then I poked his arm and he woke up in the dampness and shivered back into his slicker. I told him I could feel time folding in on me, that I felt like a very old woman, with another spring coming, more dawns to swallow up all the nights. I said I didn't know if I could stand another summer coming around. "Joe, what did you do with my mother?" I said.

He walked over to the side of the house. "I always liked this door," he said, and he put his palm flat to the wood. He pushed open the door and I followed him inside. We stood in the dark living room, listening to the rain in the fireplace. "This house," he whispered, "this house . . ."

I smelled his wet slicker and the oil. The house seemed an entirely different shape with him standing there. I imagined his sisters chasing him around, teasing him in Italian, and his parents playing cards in the kitchen with their friends.

"Christmas Eve, we always lit candles in here," he said.

I moved close to him and put my head on his damp arm.

He didn't move away and I prayed the lights would never be turned on.

"My mother used to lie on the couch in here when she was sick," he whispered. "She wouldn't take off her shoes, though, she thought the devil would take them."

"Who are you talking to?" Kate suddenly yelled from the bedroom.

"Nobody," I called, putting my hand up to Joe's lips. "Nothing, I'll be right there, now good night."

"Good night yourself," called Kate. "What are you doing in there, having a bachelor party?"

"I just want to see the kitchen," whispered Joe, and he kissed my hand.

A second later Kate was out of bed and the three of us were all bumping into one another in the dark. I felt Joe's hand brush my breast, then Kate flicked on the light.

"It's you," she said. "I thought you were a burglar cat." She stood with her hand on the light switch, decked out in her bathing cap and flannel nightgown.

"I just came by to see if you girls were O.K. by yourselves." We all stood blinking at one another in a clump against the wall. "You want me to tuck you in?" he said.

"What?" I said.

"Kate, I was talking to Kate."

"No boys allowed," she said.

I took Kate's hand. "I'll be back in a second. Now good night."

But Kate pulled away and stood between Joe and me. "You want a tour?" she said. As she walked ahead with her arm in the air like a museum guide, Joe reached out and stroked the top of my head.

"The master bedroom," said Kate, flicking on the light

in Mrs. Flax's room. We all stood staring at the double bed. The white knobby bedspread was mussed. The top drawer of her bureau was open and stockings were hanging out, and a snarl of high heels was spilling out of the closet. The whole place smelled of some new, dangerous perfume.

Joe started to have a coughing fit and I snapped off the light. Then we moved on to Joe's old room, the Red Sox room, which was still crowded with boxes. He stood rubbing his finger on the keyhole. "My sisters used to look through here," he said.

A car drove in the driveway and we all froze. Then Kate started jumping up and down, and Joe shouted, "Your mother," as he bolted for the back door.

"Kate," I yelled, "get back in bed right now!" and I ran to the front door. Kate stood right in front of me as the headlights glared on the porch. I prayed it wasn't Mrs. Flax back early to arrest me for being in the house with Joe or to arrest Joe for being there to see me and not her. Then the car started backing out of the driveway, as Joe ran off in the rain. It must have been someone who made a wrong turn.

"Dear Lord," I prayed, "give me strength to leave this town before Mrs. Flax does."

The next morning Kate got up early to go to swim practice, and I lay in bed, dreaming of Joe. At ten-thirty I walked out onto the porch in my nightgown. The rain had stopped and another spring was in the air. There was no sign of anything from the night before, no boot print, no soft orchid petals strewn across the floor, no locks of hair or scented letters.

I was out in the yard, hugging one of the wet pine trees,

when a shiny gray station wagon drove in the driveway. It was polished, the way not many people in Grove bothered to polish a station wagon. The car came right up to the porch steps, and when Mrs. Flax stepped out, I realized the car was the local taxi, which nobody I knew had ever used in their life.

Mrs. Flax dragged her suitcase behind her, bumping up the steps, and dropped it flat on the porch.

"Rained out?" I said. "What happened? Are you all right? What happened?"

"Absolutely nothing," she said. "I was bored in Pennsylvania and I was bored in Baltimore and I finally told that baseball man I was bored with him. I took a bus home, and here I am." She sat down on the swing.

"Didn't he care?"

"He cares about Astroturf, dear. It's going to ruin the game and Western civilization, according to him, and if you ever want to find yourself a boyfriend, you better start caring, too."

"Maybe it would be different once you got to Florida," I said, pushing her on the swing.

"Have you been having nightmares again? You look tired. I really have to get out of Grove. This doesn't squeak anymore."

The sun was gleaming on the grass. It was going to be one of those clear March days that made me want to tell her I was in love, and I almost leaned over and kissed her on the head.

Mrs. Flax pushed her feet against the porch, then put her legs straight out like a child. "Lou wondered what you planned to do with your life."

I stopped pushing the swing. I walked to the far end of

the porch. Fat little buds were knotted all over the trees, waiting to make their grand entrances into the world. "I'm deciding next week," I said.

"Is 'nun' still on your list? I know Lou was flirting with that young waitress in Baltimore. He was so obvious, young thing not old enough to have stretch marks. He can go straight to hell as far as I'm concerned."

I went inside but I could hear her talking to herself. "I'm sick of gardens," she said. "I'm sick of the out-of-doors. I want to live in a city where there's not all this weather and trees. I think we'll move to a city. The girls could use a little culture, and we'd get away from that baseball man." Then she called to me. "Charlotte, what about typing? It certainly has helped me over the years."

I climbed onto Kate's bunk and stared at the picture of my father's shoes. Sometimes I thought if I looked at the picture quickly enough, a mystical inspiration would pour through me like a star shooting through the galaxy, but all I noticed was that the shoes were beginning to fade.

14

❧

EVERY YEAR, for as long as the Protectors of the Blessèd Souls had stood on top of the hill in Grove, there was an Easter egg hunt on the Saturday before Easter for all the children in town. When Mrs. Flax read about the event in the local newspaper, she stood in the center of the kitchen and said firmly, "Somehow I can't see crawling around looking for hard-boiled eggs." On Easters before, in other towns, I hid bunches of jelly beans around the house when she was out.

When Mrs. Flax read the notice for the Easter egg hunt, she threw the newspaper into the garbage can. I never imagined she would change her mind, but on Saturday morning, the day of the festivities, out of the blue she woke up and said to us, "Put on your Easter bonnets, girls."

Cars were parking all over the road at the bottom of the hill and doors were slamming while we took turns zipping each other up. Kate insisted on wearing a red dress that clashed with her hair. I wore a short-sleeved dress even though it was still cool out because I wanted to show off my arms. I pinched my cheeks for color and tried to keep my eyes open as wide as I could. I wanted to be the most gorgeous woman on the planet Earth, so gorgeous that Joe would kneel in front of the whole town and beg me to run away and live in a tepee with him. Mrs. Flax wore a flowery print number and put a strange yellow bow in her hair. When we were all ready, about to step onto the porch, she stopped at the front door and put the back of her hand to her forehead.

"I can't," she said. "Easter depresses me. I hate rabbits, Peter Cottontail — the whole bit depresses me." And she pulled the ribbon out of her hair.

"It's just the nuns up there," I said. "And candy. There won't be any rabbits, don't worry about it." I picked up the ribbon off the floor and tied it around my head like a warrior.

"O.K., girls, the little family at the bottom of the hill is going hunting," said Mrs. Flax. "But I wish the whole town wasn't parked in our living room."

We stepped out onto the porch and watched families straining up the hill in their pastel clothes. They were insisting that balmy weather had arrived even though there were still patches of snow on the ground. The women carried white pocketbooks and the men wore pale sport jackets. It was true that there were traces of lime shadows on the trees, but spring was still in its teasing stage. For a moment I felt so lonely I was tempted to hold Mrs. Flax's hand, but I stepped down the porch steps, locking my hands tightly behind my back.

We threaded into the crowd swaying up the hill, and when we saw Lou and Mr. and Mrs. Crain halfway there, Mrs. Flax picked up the pace, steering us right over to them.

"Why hello, Louis." She practically curtsied. "Did you have fun down South?"

Lou gave a fake smile as he touched Kate's curls. "You girls ready to find all the eggs?"

Mary's parents were behind us and I waited to say hello. Mrs. O'Brien looked about one hundred years older than Mrs. Flax as she smiled and said, "I'm sorry Mary Elizabeth isn't here today, but she has a babysitting job she couldn't miss."

"That's nice," I said. I happened to know that Mary wasn't babysitting at all, that she was out having oral sex by the old railroad trestle with her good friend Larry. I knew she wasn't babysitting at all. The week before, while we sat eating oranges after gym class, she'd chewed on a rind and said, "It's best when they groan, don't you think?"

When we all reached the top of the hill, the convent gate was wide open. I wanted to close it and strum the bars like a harp, shouting to the townspeople that they were not allowed to enter the sacred grounds, but I walked right on in with the rest of the mob. Mother Superior was standing at the entrance, greeting everyone like a hostess, holding out Easter baskets for the children. "She looks like a black rabbit," whispered Mrs. Flax. I didn't want a basket, though. I wanted Joe. I wanted to run to the bell tower and ring the bell to make everyone go home. The convent looked so different with everyone standing nervously around, trying to be good, scared the nuns could read their minds. I looked around for Joe, pinching my cheeks every few seconds. Carrie the Avon lady was there with her three daughters. The oldest, who was a year ahead of Kate at school, had hair dyed the same orange color as Carrie's. I heard Carrie say to one of her girls, who looked about ten, "Virginity is your trump card, so save it, dear."

I wanted to tell Carrie what I knew about Joe, that he'd never made anybody in the whole world pregnant, not even me. Mrs. Flax was leaning with her back against a tree, flirting with Lou. I thought if she'd just marry Lou once and for all, then maybe she'd keep her hands off Joe. I imagined an outdoor wedding, at night, at the convent, with lights dangling from the trees. I could be a bridesmaid and Kate would be the flower girl, then when nobody was looking I'd dance away down the hill with Joe. I looked out around the pond, but there was no sign of him anywhere; I imagined him staring down at me from the bell tower and I retied the ribbon around my head.

It was a perfect day for an Easter egg hunt, as Mr. Crain kept saying to everyone, pretending he was master of ceremonies, as if he'd invented Easter egg hunts the day he was born. The forsythia buds were about to explode and curl yellow along the paths. The pond was swelling up around the spongy banks, staining everyone's spring shoes, and everyone pretended not to notice. Purple and yellow crocuses were poking up, and the combination of everyone's bright clothes and the nuns' black robes made the Easter egg hunt look like some kind of medieval pageant.

Mother Superior called all the children over to the edge of the pond to explain the rules. Kate went and stood with the other kids as they clung together around Mother Superior's plump hands. I couldn't tell if Mother Superior was missing her brother or Lou right then, but I realized she was always missing one of them every single second and was probably missing both of them at once.

I thought I heard Joe's voice, but when I turned around I realized Mr. and Mrs. Crain were snapping at each other, having an argument on holy ground that could just as well have taken place in their bedroom or in the front seat of the car. The words weren't clear, but for a moment it looked like Mrs. Crain was going to smack her husband right there in front of everyone. Then Mr. Crain said in a calm voice, as if he was addressing his constituents, although only I was listening, "You'll have to excuse us, folks, we'll be heading home now." As he took his wife by the hand, I had the distinct feeling they'd never held hands before.

I heard Joe's voice. Then I saw him, over behind some trees, talking with Carrie now. I could see her poke a finger at Joe's chest. I couldn't breathe, I was so jealous. I walked away from everyone as quickly as I could, fast, to the path around the pond. Children's laughter scattered across the water as I tried not to cry. As soon as I was far enough away I began to run, over the bridge on the far side of the pond, then deeper, back into the dark woods. I could feel my heart pounding. A substitute gym teacher in Oregon once told our class that there was a famous runner who had been badly burned in a fire as a child. He wasn't able to walk because of the pain, but if he ran fast enough the pain went away. I ran as fast as I could, and the Easter giggles of the children echoed across the pond.

I stood panting at the door of the nuns' dormitory and put my ear against the thick wood; I heard nothing. There was nobody else around. As I pushed the door open, sunlight streamed through the windows just like it was supposed to. I walked silently down the aisle between the rows of beds, pretending I had a divine aura radiating from my soul. There were about twenty beds against each wall, most of them naked pinstriped mattresses. Wooden crosses were tacked above each one. At the far end were six beds covered with black blankets, where the remaining nuns slept. Black habits hung on hooks like bat wings.

I lay down on one of the black-blanketed beds, then

put my hands together on my chest and prayed I would forget every inch of Joe Peretti. I wanted to forget every word he'd said, every burning-leaf smell of him, every breath. I prayed that some day I'd have enough strength to take the vows of poverty, chastity, and obedience. A breeze blew through the dormitory, and I wanted to stay on the bed until I fell asleep. I wanted to wake up and be a nun. I would wash in icy water, then put on the rough black robes. I would walk silently, pensively, as holy as could be, through the dormitory. I would walk along the paths to the chapel at dawn. I would be holy; I would be pure; I would not want to kill Joe Peretti because I loved him so much.

Then I jumped up and ran back into the woods, far away from the crowds.

I lay down on the damp moss behind the hedges. The dark green was comforting, not like yellow Oklahoma with all the dust. One day in Oklahoma I was sent home from school because I had been licking the chalk off the blackboard. First they sent me to the nurse, and then home, and my tongue was yellow for a long time. I had read that some young girl in the Middle Ages had visions after licking a wall, and I thought a blackboard was close enough. My teacher wrote home a note, saying that I might have mental problems. That yellow color of my chalky tongue was the color I remembered from Oklahoma, and this deep wet-moss green was Grove.

I lay on my back and shut my eyes, and soon I felt somebody standing next to me. I opened my eyes to see Joe Poseidon.

"I'm a cowboy from the Wild West," I said. "I left my mare out back. Sardinia is her name. When I ride her I spin my lasso like I'm spinning gold, and we gallop for days through the fields and up into the mountains. In winter we see the ranches in the valley, the walls all covered with snow. I'm a cowboy and when I'm cold I climb inside Sardinia and we race down the mountains. When I was a kid, my sister and I rode our horses to school or we skied. I whittled my first pair of skis, sitting with my back against the barn door. I'd whittle for hours, while my sister built little houses with the wood shavings at my feet. We carried lunch pails to school, full of jam sandwiches and fresh hunks of cheese and large triangles of berry pie."

"I miss my sisters," said Joe, but I kept talking.

"In summer we used to raft down the rivers and I played the banjo. Sometimes we swam ashore to pick flowers or lie out in the sun. We didn't have friends because the nearest ranch was a hundred miles away. We slept out, and my mother told us the stars were waiting in their places like ballerinas."

"You're going to get all wet, lying there," said Joe.

I followed him up to the bell tower, and we looked down on all the nuns surrounded by clusters of townspeople, like ants in the middle of flowers.

"You can ring the bell when it's time, if you want," said Joe Poseidon, and I stood up and he showed me how to pull the bell rope and to keep the bell from ringing too many times. I rang the bell and the visitors immediately began to draw away from the nuns, the pinks and yellows falling away from the long black robes on the wet grass, as if they were relieved to be going back into the world.

When I got home, Kate was standing in front of the fire, crying, with tears dripping down into the flames.

"Coach is gone," said Kate.

"What?" I said, pulling off my damp clothes. "What do you mean, Coach is gone?"

"She went away with Mrs. Crain, that's what Mom said. They kiss each other on the lips," said Kate, wiping her face with her sleeve.

"Who told you this?"

Kate sobbed. "And now I don't have a coach and they don't think they'll get another one this year."

It was difficult for me to get the complete story from Kate, and when I knocked on Mrs. Flax's door, she said I couldn't come in. She did say through the closed door that what Kate had said was true, that Lou had just called and said that Mr. Crain was crying for the first time since Birdie Tebbetts got traded to the Cleveland Indians. Mrs. Flax said it was true that Mr. Crain's beloved wife, who looked like a man, had been having a relationship with Coach for years, and that wasn't all. Mrs. Crain had practically been living over at Coach's house. Mr. Crain told this news to Lou, who called Mrs. Flax, who told me through the bedroom door, and Mrs. Flax said Mrs. Crain even had special shelves in the refrigerator at Coach's house. And now they were both gone. Coach had been the one to tell Mr. Crain. She called him on the telephone from a truck stop out on the highway, and she also told him that he would never be a politician or anything or anybody in the whole world, plus she said he was a lousy teacher. Mrs. Flax said she didn't think she had to throw that in, that things were bad enough. Then she went on to say that Lou had also told her that on the telephone Coach kept calling Mrs. Crain her "housemate," which made Mr. Crain so angry he had pulled the phone out of the wall.

So there wasn't any more news, except that his wife would not be coming home for dinner.

Then Mrs. Flax came out of her room and sat on the couch with a pillow on her lap.

Kate and I stood in front of the fire with our backs to Mrs. Flax.

"A kid in school's uncle was burned up and sprinkled in their garden, but I want to be sprinkled in the ocean," said Kate. "Do they really kiss each other on the lips?"

"Saint Margaret of Antioch lived as a shepherdess and was swallowed by a dragon, which burst," I said.

"Girls, stop," said Mrs. Flax.

"D'you want to sing something?" I said.

"Yes, let's sing," said Mrs. Flax. "That's a good idea." And she started to hum "I've Been Working on the Railroad."

"I don't care if a fish eats me," said Kate. "I could live inside a fish with an angel guard like Jonah."

"But it might not be one whale with a whole living room inside. You could end up in someone's tuna sandwich," I said.

"Do you think she'll write me a letter?" Kate said.

"Girls, sometimes I think I'm not your mother."

Mrs. Flax threw her pillow on the floor and went back into her room.

"Remember that guy who came over for dinner once, who took off his shirt at dinner like we were running a nudist colony?" I said to Kate, who lay down on the floor to practice her inverted side-stroke kick.

The only time we were close to having someone naked at the dinner table, which I was always waiting to see after looking at a brochure on nudist colonies that once arrived in the mail, was when Mrs. Flax had this man over for dinner one night in Texas. He kept scaring Kate by pretending to take quarters out of her ears. He told us he was a magician, but later Mrs. Flax told us he didn't know his ass from his elbow. It was a very hot night and in the middle of the meal the guy said, "I don't want to ruin my shirt." I couldn't tell if he meant from sweating because it was so hot or from spilling something, but he unbuttoned his shirt and hung it on the back of his chair. It began to lightning and thunder, with rain streaming down the screens. Kate put down her baby fork and stared at the man's hairy stomach. About a minute later she slid down from her high chair and crawled away from the table.

But Kate said she didn't know what I was talking about, that she didn't remember any man without a shirt, taking quarters out of her ears, and she continued to lie on the floor crying.

"How about 'Oh What a Beautiful Morning'?" I got the record of *Oklahoma* and put it on the record player. I turned it up loud and placed the needle down on the song. Mrs. Flax sang along from her bedroom because we both knew it usually made Kate smile. But Kate covered her ears with her hands. About halfway through the record, it began to skip — "Oh what a beautifl, Oh what a beautifl, Oh what a beautifl" — until Mrs. Flax yelled that if I didn't turn off the record player immediately, she would throw the record and the record player out the window, so I turned it off.

I tried to cheer Kate up all afternoon, telling her about when she was a baby and telling her about when I used to read her the Bible, and once she had asked in baby talk whether Pontius Pilate was a bomber pilot. Kate didn't stop crying, though, and I reminded her of when we used to play ventriloquists. We would clamp our teeth and our lips moved around like pink worms. "Can you tell we're talking, Mom, huh, can you tell?" And Mrs. Flax would say, "I can't imagine who could be talking. There's certainly no one here but you crazy kids."

But Kate continued to cry.

Mrs. Flax emerged from her bedroom, wearing a full face of the latest make-up she had purchased from Carrie, and she bent down over Kate and petted her on the back.

"It will be all right, baby, don't worry. Would you like me to fix you some food?"

I bent down and touched Kate's hair so both of us were stroking her, trying to make her stop crying. We knelt by the fire and massaged her, whispering to her that everything would be all right, and finally her sobs got quieter and she fell asleep.

15

✵

In the days that followed, Kate spent every free moment in the swimming pool. I could tell she was doing her crying in the water because after Easter she stopped crying at home. She told me, though, if I ever mentioned Coach or how they kissed on the lips she'd throw her rock collection at me.

I spent hours lying on my bed, trying to remember Joe's lips on that November night up in the tower, and the rest of the hours trying to figure out what my father would look like in the flesh. Mrs. Flax wouldn't say one word about him, and when I pointed out that he did say he was going to be visiting in the spring and it was almost spring, that there was definitely a sweetness in the air, she asked me to please, kindly, keep quiet. What she did say when she barged into our bedroom one evening after work was, "There's a nice new lawyer at work, and I think I'd like to invite him over for dinner soon."

She even bought a bottle of sweet kosher wine and put it in the refrigerator. Well, this nice young lawyer never materialized and she went back to dating Lou. Mr. Crain didn't move in with him the way Mrs. Flax suggested, and God strike me down, but as I sat in history class one day I began to have these thoughts about Mr. Crain, and you didn't have to be from the F.B.I. to figure out I wasn't on some direct phone line to God.

What I thought, as I stared at Mr. Crain and was supposed to be learning about the New Deal, was that Mr. Crain was not a history teacher, really, but a tailor, and I imagined bringing my clothes to his tailor shop one day after school.

I imagined I was standing in front of the mirror, and he knelt down on a small pillow he kept strapped with an elastic band around his knee like a garter. He tossed the tape measure around his neck and slowly pinned up my dress, really short, taking each pin from a row he held between his lips. Then as he stood up, he lightly touched the inside of my leg.

"Wait, let me lock up," he said. "I must sweep."

He swept the floor, carefully bending down to pick up odd pins, while I hung up my purse on a stray hanger among all the cut-out men's suits.

On the counter was a bowl of tailor's chalk and another one full of lemon drops. As Mr. Crain the tailor turned the OPEN sign in the window to CLOSED, I popped a lemon drop into my mouth. Then he took a bolt of gray flannel and unwrapped it on the counter. He pointed his scissors to a length of material as if I was going to have something made, and I nodded as he swiftly cut the soft gray flannel and laid it out behind the counter on the floor.

The tailor unzipped his pants, which he had stitched himself but were slightly long. He unbuckled his belt and asked me to lie down on the gray flannel. And what I won dered, when I lay on the soft flannel, was if my father ever went to a tailor's shop and if he had enough money to have suits specially made. And I wondered what the odds would be of me lying down on the flannel and then my father coming into the shop the next day and asking the tailor to make him a suit out of the very same fabric. I knew the odds were not good, but what I really wondered was if he did walk out in a big gray flannel suit that smelled of his daughter, Charlotte Flax, would he know?

Every so often someone knocked at the door of the shop and the tailor smiled down at me behind the counter and stroked me like the smooth hull of a Greek ship.

16

A cool spring evening, when Kate was staying late at the pool and I was at the kitchen table, trying to read about the Electoral College, Mrs. Flax ran out of the house without a coat, carrying an open bag of potato chips in her hand. "El señor has returned," she yelled from the car as she drove away.

I ran out onto the porch. "Dear Lord," I said to the trees. "Dear Lord, I will sell my soul if he who has forsaken me has finally returned."

When I was young I used to see whole houses on trailers out on the highways, with red flags flying from the back, and I imagined my father lifting up the house with his hands and driving it all the way back up from Brazil or wherever he lived. "Our Father Who Art in Heaven is coming," I shouted to the trees. I could hear him say to Mrs. Flax, "And here's my long-lost daughter, Charlotte. I didn't realize you had a starlet living with you." Then I'd introduce myself and he'd ask me to autograph his handkerchief right away.

I went inside and knelt on a chair at the sink. I washed

my hair with icy water so it chilled all down my spine. I
gasped for breath and stared at myself in the sopping wet
mirror. When I squinted my eyes I thought I looked exactly like Mrs. Flax. And then I thought I looked like Joe.
When I was a kid I thought that when two people slept
together, whatever sticky stuff passed back and forth made
them look alike, which was why so many couples look alike.

I wrapped my hair in a towel and began dabbing a bunch
of Mrs. Flax's perfume behind my ears and knees. The front
door slammed and I crossed myself.

"Man overboard," yelled Kate.

I opened the bathroom door to find Kate with her
bloodshot eyes and copper-colored hair, looking mournful.
A bathing suit was hanging from each wrist.

"So where is he?" she said. "I passsed Mom on the road
and she gave me the news. Who are you, Queen of Sheba,
with that towel? Pool's closed," she said. "They're cleaning
it. I can't swim for a whole week." She sat on the edge of
the bathtub as I tried on different kinds of make-up, a
dark red lipstick and violet eyeshadow on my eyes.

"Can you hand me the shark cream?" said Kate.

As I smoothed rouge onto my cheeks, Kate sat rubbing
green crow's-feet cream on her face. I was getting too
jumpy, waiting around for Mr. Flax, and convinced Kate
to come out to the back yard with me and try to straighten
up the place.

"Is Pop going to sleep in Mom's double bed?" asked Kate
as I tried to ram the lawn mower through the grass. "That
perfume you've got on is giving me a hernia."

The lawn mower jammed, so I paced without it. It was
seven o'clock and he still hadn't shown up. I almost ran up
to the convent to tell Joe he'd arrived, but then a car

pulled in the driveway. We could hear it. The motor kept running, but it was definitely parked. As the engine stayed on, my hands began to shake. I grabbed Kate and ran in the back door, straight to our room, where we hid in the closet. I hugged Kate in the dark. I decided I'd be the most serene woman he'd ever met. I wasn't going to ask him what the hell he'd been doing all these years, or where the hell he'd been or with whom. I'd talk as sweet as sugar.

The motor was still running.

"Maybe it's not him," said Kate. "Maybe it's one of her regular boyfriends."

"No," I said. "He's just shy. She likes shy men, and he was the original shy man."

"They might be kissing on the lips," said Kate.

"You're just a little green girl," I said.

"You should talk. You look like somebody drew all over you," said Kate.

The motor turned off. A second later the car door slammed.

"Our Father Who Art in Heaven has returned to earth," I said. I was about to run out of the closet, when I heard Mrs. Flax's voice, which didn't sound any different than usual.

"Girls," she called, "where are you? Would you mind lending me your ears for a moment?"

"What?" I said, as evenly as I could, trying to sound like a Quaker woman, thinking my father was standing right outside.

"Are you all right? Where's Kate?"

"We're just cleaning the closet, Mother, thank you very much for asking."

"What the hell is going on in there?"

"Nothing, thank you, Mother."

"Look, I don't know whether this is some new religion or what, Charlotte, but I just came in to tell you I'm going out. Your father is here and we'll be back later.

"Yes, of course, Mother."

"See you girls later, and see to it that Kate eats some real food."

"Mother?" I screamed. "Mother, are you there?"

The door slammed and Kate and I pushed our way out of the closet, as the car drove off.

"She couldn't have," I whispered. "They'll be back soon. They probably just went for a little drive. We can wait on the porch." I went into the kitchen and leaned against the refrigerator. I almost cried, but I yelled, "Kate!"

"Sergeant!" Kate shouted back.

"We'll wait up all night if we have to, O.K.? We'll celebrate." I couldn't believe Mrs. Flax hadn't brought him inside first thing. Kate came into the living room wrapped in towels, with green paste still on her face and the bathing suits hanging off her wrists again.

"We could have a birthday party," she said. "We never did that." Then she turned all her trophies upside-down.

I went into Mrs. Flax's room and opened the closet door. The closet was stuffed with dresses and the floor was a clutter of high heels. I reached in and pulled out her favorite polka dot dress. "Care to dance, Mrs. Flax, Mrs. Polka Flax?" I said as I held the dress to my waist. I could hear Kate rearranging her rock collection as I unwound the towel from my head.

Kate called in, "If you're wearing one of her dresses, she'll probably kill you. D'you think I should wash these rocks?"

I unzipped the polka dot dress and pulled it on over my head. It almost fit. If I was walking along the street in some other town, wearing that dress, nobody would accuse me of wearing my mother's dress. I put my hands on my hips and spun around in front of the mirror, then picked up the towel and rubbed my hair. Then I tried on every pair of shoes, until I thought I'd broken my ankles from clacking back and forth.

"You tap dancing?" called Kate.

"I'm a woman," I said.

"She's going to kill you, she really is."

I found a pair of black patent leather heels that seemed dressy enough for the occasion. I stepped into them, then fell back on the double bed.

I shut my eyes to the sound of running water. Kate was washing the rocks. I was just going to take a little nap. If I could get through that night, I decided, I could survive anything.

When I woke up I thought I could feel the earth spinning around. I felt the silky polka dot dress on my legs and kicked my high-heeled feet together. "Kate," I called. "My child, is he here?"

I imagined going to the beach with my father. He'd hold me high above his head, walking into the ocean like we were acrobats. When the waves hit he'd hold me tight, as the salt water splashed my face. I'd hold on to his slippery shoulders, and if sand got stuck in my eye he'd quickly stick out his tongue and lick it away.

I jumped up and fell off the high heels, then slowly tottered down the hall. Kate was in our room, drying off the rocks with toilet paper.

"He'll love those," I said, pointing to the rocks. "You ready to celebrate?"

Kate slowly put her rocks back on the shelf, then took down the fish encyclopedia and opened it upside-down on her head. "She's going to kill you in that," she said.

"Cute hat," I said. "It that what you plan to wear?" Along with the book on her head, Kate was wearing a dress she wore to school, nothing fancy, with up-and-down red stripes and a little bit of grape jelly on the collar.

Kate went out to the porch swing to wait, while I went to the kitchen to invent a party. I opened the refrigerator, singing "We Three Kings of Orient Are," and surveyed the rations.

There was a silver-papered rectangle of fairly new cream cheese, jars of mushrooms, pickles, little onions, olives, and a bottle of red wine stuck against a jar of strawberry jam. There were also plates covered with wax paper that I didn't want to know about. I took out the wine, cream cheese, and olives, then set them out on the kitchen table. I got a loaf of bread from the bread box and tried to calm myself by lining up the food alphabetically. "Celebrate," I said out loud. "It's not the Last Supper, but it will have to do."

Actually, what I decided to make was sandwiches. Most people wouldn't write home about sandwiches, but Kate and I thought they were the most exotic things around, because we rarely saw them in their natural form. Mrs. Flax was always cutting them up into microscopic triangles or stupid cookie-cutter shapes, so a real sandwich, two rectangles you could hold in your hands was sort of like Mardi Gras for us.

I forked out ten olives and sucked out all the pimientos, because Kate always said they gave her hernias. I wasn't wild about them either, so I spit them, red and wet, into the sink. I made a stack of cream cheese and olive sandwiches and, with my hands still shaking, poured two glasses of sweet wine as neatly as I could.

We weren't big drinkers. Even Mrs. Flax, aside from New Year's Eve, rarely had a drink, and if she drank at home it was a big event. We didn't normally keep much liquor in the house, except for one dusty bottle of vodka in the back of the broom closet, which Mrs. Flax only very occasionally took out and mixed with warm ginger ale. When she did she always said, "I am going to have a drink now, girls," very slowly, as if she were reading a sign written in block letters with large nursery school crayons. "I am going to have a drink."

"You want a drink?" I called to Kate.

"Juice," she yelled. "Do we have any juice?"

I looked in the refrigerator again, but there still wasn't any juice. I balanced the plate of sandwiches on my arm and walked with the two glasses of wine straight ahead of me. I tried not to spill too much as I laid out the feast on the porch in front of Kate.

"Happy Birthday, Fish Head," I said.

Kate crossed her legs like a grown-up, took a sip of wine, and sputtered like a cat. "This is disgusting," she said as the encyclopedia crashed to the floor.

We each took about two bites of sandwich, but it didn't mix well with the wine. "Can I freshen your drink, my love," I said, standing up. My legs felt warm, like they belonged to somebody else.

"Charmed, I'm sure," said Kate. "I'll stay here and watch the kids."

"Those kids can be so much trouble," I said. I took our glasses and tripped on the high heels back to the kitchen. I swear it felt like the wine was poured directly into my feet. I filled up the glasses again, then found an old tray that Mrs. Flax had painted from a paint-by-numbers kit. It was supposed to be a picture of a bowl of fruit, but she had insisted the numbers were the same on all the fruit, so she'd painted the oranges, apples, bananas, and grapes all blue. I remembered her using the tray only once, when she had one of her bosses over for dinner. She'd served coffee on the tray, and when she brought it to the table she put her hand on the boss's shoulder and laughed, saying something about the paint-by-numbers people not having their heads screwed on right.

I stood the glasses on the tray, then balanced it on one hand like a waiter. I walked to the door, kicking it open ahead of me, then held the tray high above Kate's head.

"Charmed, I'm sure," said Kate as I lowered the tray. "What lovely blue fruit." And she took a glass.

"A toast," I said. "A toast to living forever."

"Forever and the sea," said Kate. We clinked glasses three times and the wine sloshed up and spilled pink over our hands.

"On your mark, get set, go!" I said. We raced to see who could finish first. Kate won, holding her nose as she drank. When she finished she put the bottom of her glass up to her eye like a telescope and looked at me. "After you swim the Channel, they always give you champagne," she said.

She picked up a sandwich, opened it up, and calmly pulled out the olives. She ate those, then dropped the bread and cream cheese down on the plate. "Charmed, I'm sure," she said.

17

꧁

WE SAT looking for headlights in the dark, getting dizzy and drunk on the swing. It was a cool night, with the pine trees dancing around in front of the house. I put my arm around Kate and swung higher, telling her about the day she was born. Mrs. Flax had held her up to the hospital window and I'd waved from the street. I swear I remember Kate waving back, even though she was only half a day old.

"You're not going to run away again, are you?" said Kate.

"You want to walk up to the convent?" I said.

"I thought you wanted to say hello to Pop."

"He'll be here when we get back. I don't want him thinking we don't have anything better to do than wait around all our lives for him."

I helped Kate up. We grabbed hands, wobbling down the porch steps, laughing into the night. Then Kate stood in the middle of the yard, doing an excellent imitation of Carrie. "Know your colors and know your fabrics, that's what I tell my little girls." Then she reached up and pinched my cheek.

We began to walk up the hill, laughing, toward the convent. We took turns pushing each other from the back, giggling and giggling in the dark breeze.

"Shush, shush," I said. "Be careful or we'll wake up the nuns." And then we laughed some more.

When we reached the top of the hill, I put my arm around Kate and kissed the back of her neck. "You're mental," she said as she squirmed around.

When we got to the gate, I pulled her to her knees on the moss. "Remember I told you I once saw the nuns playing horseshoes? Well, I also saw them playing basketball. They were laughing, and as they ran around, their habits sailed up and I saw their black starched underwear, I swear to God."

The evening bell began to ring up in the tower. I looked up to see if Joe had lit a candle, the way he sometimes did, but it was pitch dark. The bell rang on and on, until it felt like the bell was inside me, ringing from my heart. "He's back," I whispered. "He's back, he's back." I turned to my sister.

"Kate, my love?"

"Sergeant?" Kate hiccupped from her knees.

"You want to go up in the bell tower?"

"I'd fall off," she said as she tipped over onto the moss.

"Come on up," I said, pulling her to her feet. "You've never been up, have you?"

"You're going up there in those shoes?" said Kate, hiccupping some more.

"C'mon up," I said, pulling her by the arm.

"No, I'm going to look for some new rocks."

"I'll be right back," I said.

"Act your age, not your shoe size." She waved.

I let go of her, and then I ran as fast as I could to the tower. I turned my ankle and stopped and waved in the dark. Then I climbed the steps three at a time.

"Joe," I whispered. The bell had stopped and I couldn't see a thing. "Joe, you here?" I stumbled around, then fell into his lap.

"What? Is that perfume? Have you been drinking?"

"Kiss me and we'll both know," I said. I put my lips on his lips and threw my arms around his neck.

He didn't stop me. He slid his arms around me and quickly pulled down the zipper of the polka dot dress. I once explained to Kate that sometimes if you kiss someone nothing happens, the way it is when you kiss your own hand, or when Kate climbed onto the sink in the bathroom and began kissing herself in the mirror. But sometimes, I explained to Kate — and Kate had jumped up and down and said, "I know, sometimes there's chemicals," and gave one of her little maniac grins.

Well, with Joe there were chemicals. He pulled off his sweater and shirt and I breathed in his warm chest. I was kissing his arms when he took off my underwear. He slid inside me and I held on tight as he filled me up. I thought I'd lost my breath forever, as if a great bird had fallen from my feet. And then it was over; we were virgins no more. I sat collapsed on his lap, while he traced the white vaccination on my thigh from when I was a baby, a hazy spot like the moon when you know it will rain the next day. I put my head on his shoulder and whispered, "Mea culpa, mea culpa." Joe and I clung together in a cloud of Mrs. Flax's perfume, and then we heard splashing, like Kate had hurled her whole rock collection into the pond.

We scrambled for our clothes. As I twisted my arms back to zip up Mrs. Flax's polka dot dress, Mother Superior started shrieking at the top of her lungs. "Joe, Joe, come quickly, Joseph!" We didn't get there as fast as we should, but finally Joe was able to run down the stone steps, and I stumbled down right behind.

Down at the pond Mother Superior was swinging around her black umbrella and a flashlight like some sort of deranged lighthouse. I couldn't see what was going on, just the ripples of water and clusters of leaves where the flashlight shone. Joe ran to the tool shed, and all I could say was, "Where's my sister Kate, you know, Reverend Mother, have you seen my sister?"

There were nuns, more nuns than I'd ever seen at the convent, running around with their hands up in the air. A police car showed up, then everybody began talking about calling the fire department. The water was icy, everybody knew it was, but everyone kept repeating it over and over like it was news, and twice Mother Superior asked a policeman if he thought an umbrella would help.

I walked away, my high heels sinking into the moss off the path, and I vomited into the woods. I threw my arms around the nearest tree, holding on as tightly as I could. "Jesus Christ, find my sister."

It was the teenage nun, the one I'd seen last year at the shoe store, who swam out in the dark and found her. I couldn't move from the edge of the pond and stood hugging myself while Mother Superior ran back to her cottage to call Mrs. Flax.

Kate was so pale, with splotches of green shark paste still on her cheeks, with her curly red hair and her watery blue eyes. She was draped over the nun's arms like a little striped fish, in that dress of hers, and everyone kept saying,

"Is she still breathing? Is she still breathing?" like they had speech problems. I walked over to her and kissed her wet curls. Then quickly there were all sorts of policemen and nuns putting her in the back of the police car, although I could have easily lifted her by myself. As they drove off to the hospital, I stood alone at the edge of the pond. I don't know where Joe had gone, but I could see Mother Superior pacing under the willow trees, fingering the silver cross on her chest. Her wimple was crooked on her head. I wanted to tell Kate it seemed like we were in some haunted movie, and I held my palms together tightly, chanting, "Kate, Kate, Kate."

I stayed up at the convent all night, kneeling at the wooden crucifix in the pines, with my hands holding Christ's wooden ankles. I prayed that Kate would be all right, and I prayed that Mrs. Flax wouldn't shoot me, and I prayed that my father wouldn't make me walk the plank as soon as we said how-do-you-do. Some time that night the firemen showed up, with sirens blaring, but somebody must have clued them in because they left as soon as they arrived.

When Mother Superior finally got hold of Mrs. Flax, it was almost the next day. The famous Mr. Flax was not with her because it turned out they had staged a preview of World War III out at the motel at the edge of town and he had gone away again.

The next day was a bright, sunny, cruel day, with baby birds chirping in a clean wind, the way God does on his best days, and I began to cry for the first time in years, dripping into the mud, crying my eyes out, as if the mud would notice and the birds would stop. I prayed that it would be dark and cold. I prayed that it would rain, but the sun continued to climb higher in the sky. If a visiting nun had walked along the paths, her skirts trailing behind, she might not have known it wasn't a normal day at all.

18

W HEN I GOT HOME with throw-up on the
dress and tears dripping through my make-up, there was
nobody there. Mrs. Flax was at the hospital, and I didn't
exactly get a written invitation. The reason I didn't just
show up was human fear. I was mainly frightened I'd killed
my little sister. I was also scared out of my mind that if
anybody saw me I'd be immediately sent to some kind of
juvenile delinquent school, where I'd wear a faded gray
jumper the rest of my life and eat at a long narrow table
next to hoody girls who carried switchblades in their knee
socks. And I was petrified that this time I really did have a
Joey, Jr., rolling around inside me, and the juvenile delinquent school would only give my baby one ripped doll to
play with.

So I spent the day alone in the house. I spent hours in the
shower, scrubbing off the make-up and the perfume and
crying into the kitchen sink, with tears dripping over the
red pimentos that lay in the drain, and when I wasn't in the
shower, screaming and crying, I was crying everywhere
else. I sat at the kitchen table, with my head down, crying
into my arms, and I cried in every room of the house.

That night Mrs. Flax didn't call or come home, and I climbed onto the top bunk and hugged Kate's chlorine-smelling pillow.

I waited for Kate to come home. I waited for her to run in and hang her wet bathing suits on the bedpost, then climb up onto the top bunk with her latest library book of fish in her mouth. I waited for her to empty her pockets all over the floor and spill out a new pile of stones for her rock collection, and I waited for her to start jabbering about the latest kick she had learned. I would have said, "You'll be the fastest person in the Channel, faster than the sharks," which is what she always asked me to say. I waited for her to prance in, wearing one of her little dresses, with her bathing cap on her head, and say, "I swam all the way to Nevada today, I really did." And I would tell her to get her wet bathing cap off before she caught cold.

I fell down from the top bunk twice and wanted to permanently bruise myself, and when I realized I was still alive I stood up and took one of Kate's bathing suits from the bedpost and wrapped it around my neck like a scarf. Then I turned all the swim trophies right side up that Kate had turned over, and I dusted them even though they weren't dusty at all.

I screamed at the ceiling, "What is this, anyway, some kind of pop quiz, God?" and I kept the windows tightly shut, trying to keep out spring, which was coming in right on schedule with a taunting breeze.

I lay on Kate's bunk as the house got hot, and I remembered playing with her on a summer night in Texas. We'd taken off our shirts and thrown them on the ground, and I'd raced with Kate bouncing up and down on my shoulders, her baby legs curling smooth around my neck.

Suddenly I was starving and I jumped down from the top

bunk and went to the kitchen. I boiled up a bunch of plain spaghetti, in honor of Kate. Then I threw a handful at the refrigerator door, crying the whole time, talking to Kate, trying to joke about how we could never remember if the strands stuck when spaghetti was ready or when it wasn't.

Once the phone rang but I was scared to answer it, and I imagined it was Kate at school after swim practice, and she said, "Hello, dahlink," in a water-logged Zsa Zsa Gabor voice. "Do you think you could send the chauffeur to pick me up at zee spa?"

And then I picked up the empty wine bottle and threw it against the refrigerator door, against the stray strands of spaghetti, so it crashed and splintered to the floor.

Finally I exhausted myself and staggered back to bed, but I should have gotten a rain check for that sleep. I had the kind of nightmare people in prison probably have every single night.

I dreamed Kate drowned and was as dead as a human person can be. And then we burned her up. The funeral was held at the pool at school, which they'd almost finally finished refilling. Lou wore a real suit, but his shoes were splattered with paint. He kept putting his hand up in the air to block the sun through the windows. It was hot inside, steamy hot, the way the pool always was, and I saw Kate in her turquoise bathing suit at the edge of the pool, ready to fly into the water. Mr. Crain was there, holding in his stomach and shuffling his baseball cards. Carrie stood next to him, wearing a black chiffon scarf around her neck and crying into a black handkerchief. She reminded me of a joke Kate liked, about a woman who wore a black ribbon around her neck, and one day when she finally took off the ribbon her head fell off.

I don't know who chose him, but Mr. Crain gave the

eulogy as he continued to shuffle the baseball cards. He began with part of a speech about democracy that he'd probably composed years before, and when he finally got around to talking about Kate's innocent life, and everybody was staring into the half-filled pool, Mother Superior pushed open the heavy door and walked in. She walked right up to Lou, and I really couldn't tell through my tears, but she might have put her hand on his arm. I stood as close as I dared to Mrs. Flax, but still she hadn't spoken an English word to me.

As soon as Mr. Crain pointed to me and asked me to say a few words, I woke up from the nightmare, screaming and panting for breath. The sun was glaring in the windows. My day of reckoning had arrived.

I had to get to the hospital. I jumped out of bed and ran outside. The hospital was two towns away. I started walking on a pilgrimage to save my soul. I had marched for about twenty minutes, swearing at the birds to keep quiet, when Joe drove by the other way in his brown car. He did a U-turn in the middle of the road, then drove slowly along, following me.

"Get in the car," he said, leaning out the window.

I kept walking and he kept driving along.

"Will you please get in the car?" he said. "There's somebody behind me."

"I don't care if there's a motorcade behind you, I have to get to the hospital."

"I was just there. She's going to be O.K."

"What?" I stopped.

"Please," said Joe, and he reached over and opened the door.

I got in when the car behind him started honking. He was wearing a black suit and a stiff white shirt with cuffs that stuck out the sleeves like large bandages around his wrists. And that was the exact second — when I saw his cuffs — that was the moment I knew I wouldn't fall over if I couldn't be with him for the rest of my life. He looked different. I couldn't tell if he looked older or younger, but he'd changed. We drove far out of town. Gangs of cows were wandering the green hills, with their bells ringing like buoys in the ocean.

"She's exhausted, and she has to stay there a couple more days, but she's going to be O.K."

I stuck my head out the window and thanked God.

"What did you once tell me about white gravy?" asked Joe.

"Tell you what?"

"You know, you and Kate."

"Nothing. Just once when we were in Oklahoma at a coffee shop, she wanted white gravy and biscuits like they eat there, and when she got the food she poured the gravy all over her head."

As Joe stepped on the gas, I noticed he was still wearing his moccasins. We rode along silently, and I remembered his hand on my thigh.

"Look," he said, "I've got to get away from here. I'm going to stay with my sisters in Florida for a while. Maybe you could visit sometime, I mean if you want to."

I think the cows had heard more passionate declarations of love, but it was the closest he'd ever gotten to saying he cared, and I touched his hand on the steering wheel.

Mrs. Flax and I arrived back at the house at just about the same time. We stood on the porch in the sunlight, squinting at each other. When she raised her hand to hit me, I raised my hand to stop her. We stood there forever, like we were about to do a jump ball, and I realized as I stared into her eyes that I'd grown a little taller than her, not like I was a female giant or anything, but a little taller. Then I said something like, "I guess her angel guard was watching over her," and we both smiled and lowered our hands. We stood talking in half sentences on the sunny porch, and I suggested we stay in Grove, maybe for another year.

My mother said she was worn out, and that although staying put was against her rules of life, the thought of packing up the car again made her weak in the knees. Then we hugged quickly, and I could feel us both begin to cry.

19

STAYING PUT is the hardest thing we've ever done. It's been two months now. Flowers are strewn like constellations over the hills just the way nature does it every year. It seems we will stay, at least for a while.

Kate really does seem to be O.K. She gets a little dizzy sometimes, but the doctor says that will pass. He has asked her to stay out of the water for a few more weeks, which I think she'll be able to do. She just does double time in the bathtub, which she doesn't seem to mind. For a while she said she didn't want me to borrow her *Fish of the World* book ever, but just last night she said if *she* held the book and turned the pages, leaning over from the top bunk, and I sat on my bed, she'd show me the pictures.

I take a lot of walks at dawn, when the grass is still wet. Joe's gone, but he's been sending me postcards, the same ones his sister used to send him, with the palm trees, and he's thinking of opening a greenhouse with one of his brother-in-laws. He said he'd come up to snowshoe in the winter, and I really think he will.

There's been plenty of gossip, in case you wondered. I

can almost feel people's words dripping off their collars as I pass. Even Mary O'Brien thinks I was pretty wild, doing it with a guy almost twice my age. She figured it all out; don't ask me how. My mother's been talking about sending me to some kind of a guidance counselor. That's on hold for now though, because ever since Mrs. Crain went off with Coach, the P.T.A. voted not to hire a new counselor for at least another year.

Last Tuesday was my birthday and I skipped school. I mean, classes are almost over, and when something like this happens, one more or less class on the Panama Canal really doesn't matter. I drove out of town and found where Joe and I had gone sledding. I climbed the hill, then lay down and rolled over and over, down through the dizzy green grass, staring up at the sky. I thought of Kate and shouted, "I am a human bean!" and then I rolled some more.

The convent looks like it's going to go out of business soon. It's hard to tell, though. Every afternoon there's a new rumor of what they'd turn the place into. Lou's been proposing to my mother around the clock. God knows what she'll do, but she's been cooking up a storm, and Kate said she even thought she heard her say something about cooking a main course, but Kate's hearing has been fuzzy for a while.

I've gotten some new books on Greek myths from the library, and I've been reading a lot about Icarus — you know, with those melty wings and all — but I'm not going to let it get out of hand.